Family Portrait

by
John S. Lundgren

Family Portrait

Published by John S. Lundgren

ISBN: 9781655580239
Imprint: Independently published

"A family is a mystery."

Sharon Olds

Stay open to opportunities.

Better yet, *create possibilities*!

Family Portrait

by
John S. Lundgren

Intro A: Sean and Maya

It was hot in the room. Sean rolled over onto his back. The sheets were damp, and he could feel his bare skin clammy with sweat. Through bleary eyes, he spotted Maya sitting at the foot of the bed, leaning up against the post. Her sketch pad was propped up against her leg.

"What are you doing?" he asked, groggily.

"You looked so sexy, all naked and sweaty. And your butt was perfectly round. I wanted to draw it."

He rubbed his eyes.

"And then you rolled over," she added. "So, I had sketch this side too."

"Since when are you drawing again?" he asked. "I thought you were all about mixed media, collage."

"I got bored with that. And Tony was working in the studio with his shirt off, so I drew him. I hadn't done any figure drawing since art school. It felt good so I joined a workshop group. You're my extra credit."

"Let me see," he said, reaching for the pad.

"No, I'm not done."

Rebuffed, his hand fell back to his stomach, then unconsciously he touched his dick.

"Wait," she called. "Stay just like that."

He froze.

"You make a good model. Since you're not working, you could make some decent money at the school."

"No," he said emphatically. "And aren't they all huge . . . and gay?"

"They aren't all gay. You can always pose with your dick covered if you're afraid you don't measure up," she joked. "But we've seen a lot of dicks. Short, long, fat, cut and not. It's your tattoos that make you unique."

Sean had intricate tattoos on his shoulders and half-sleeves on both arms.

"It's hard to capture the detail in the ink, without losing the contour and shading in your muscles."

"So, you think, my dick is too small?" he barked. He reached for her and pulled her roughly onto him. The sketch pad fell to the side of the bed.

"I never said that," she teased. "I said you'd make a good model." He was already hard from being watched. "And I have the tits of a twelve-year boy. We're well matched."

He thrust his hips up. She gasped and followed his motion. After a short time, they came together and she fell onto his chest, kissing him. Both satisfied.

"So, I have the dick of a twelve-year-old boy?"

"I've never seen the dick of a twelve-year-old," she answered. She reached for the sketch pad, handing it to him. In the quick drawing, she had clearly given him extra credit in his size. "This should let you know I how I feel about your anatomy."

"It just looks big because of the perspective. It's in the foreground."

She kissed him again before standing up. "Just take the compliment," she said, before adding, "I've got to take a shower and get to the studio."

He rolled onto his side, watching her lean body as she padded to the bathroom.

When she returned ten minutes later, Sean had pulled on underwear and a t-shirt.

"What are you doing today?" she asked as she dressed in a lace thong, jeans and a fitted t-shirt.

"Laundry," he answered.

"Good," she said. "I don't have any clean bras. Hence . . ." she placed her hands over her t-shirt covered breasts.

"And I'll clean up around here. Vacuum. Maybe spend some time on my music."

At that last comment, she looked at him. "Any job prospects? Our savings aren't going to hold out forever."

"I'll make some more calls," he responded, sullenly.

Maya picked up her jacket, backpack and keys. "Will you be late?" Sean asked. "I'll make dinner."

"I'm not sure," she said. "I'm really focused on this figure work. I want to experiment with different media to see what I like working with." She tossed the backpack on her shoulder. "I'll let you know later. But, it's Thursday, so, when I get back from Brooklyn, let's plan on walking down to Stella's. A greasy burger, and a show at a dive bar, sounds perfect to me." She stood on her toes to reach his cheek. After a quick kiss, she whispered in his ear, "For the record, I love your dick."

11

Turning, she looked back and gave a flirty wink. "See you tonight, stud."

As the door closed, he cupped his groin. He was getting hard again.

Intro B: Greg and Constance

"What are you doing?" asked Constance as Greg pulled his British make sedan to the side of the road on their way home from dinner.

He shifted into *park* and looked to his left, out the driver's side window.

"I just love living here," he answered. "I never get tired of the changing scenery."

Remnants of winter were everywhere. Snowbanks that had been melting in the daylight was now crusted over on both sides of the street. Trees that would eventually blossom into an explosion of green lay barren. Honeycombed ice covered most of the lake. In the small area of open water along the shore, the full moon reflected brightly.

"Come on," she hurried. "You can look at the moon from home."

Greg diverted his gaze and glanced over at Constance. The shade was open on the car's sunroof and the moon illuminated her beautiful face. He knew she'd be in less of hurry if she could see herself in this flattering light. Despite the new Jag's purring engine providing plenty of warm air to the cabin, Constance pulled her designer shawl and cashmere scarf tighter to her body.

"Seriously," she implored. "I have to fly back to New York tomorrow."

"Just a minute longer," he answered, reaching out to hold her gloved hand.

She reached up to lightly stroke his soft beard. "My sweet, romantic, young husband." Smiling, she grasped his hand again and renewed her silent vow to never let him go.

A moment later, Constance cried, "What was that?"

"What?" asked Greg.

"Up across the lake. I thought I saw a flash." A moment later there was a popping sound.

"I don't know I didn't see it. Maybe a shooting star? The sky is so clear tonight."

She squeezed his hand tighter and leaned across the armrest to nuzzle into his shoulder.

Neither of them was aware of the minutes that passed when a flashing blue light interrupted their peace.

"What is that?" asked Constance.

Looking in his side mirror, Greg answered, "Looks like a police car coming up the parkway."

"No siren?"

"There's no traffic," said Greg. "Probably don't want to disturb the neighborhood."

The police cruiser passed and was followed shortly by an ambulance. Both vehicles stopped on the curve a few blocks ahead. The flash from the strobing lights made them both squint.

After another lasting look at the moon, Greg released Constance's hand, shifted the car into gear, and said, "Let's go home."

Greg slowed the car as they approached the stopped emergency vehicles.

"I wonder what's going on in there," said Constance. "I didn't think anyone lived there."

"The place belongs to an old guy," said Greg. "I saw him outside once. . .a year or two ago." After a brief pause, he added, "I've never seen anyone else there though. And I can't remember even seeing any lights on for a long time. Just a dark facade."

"He must have died. Maybe someone will do something with that house," offered Constance. "It's a disgrace how it's been allowed to deteriorate like that."

"If he is dead," said Greg, "it's sad."

"It's not like we knew him."

"Come on Connie, you know what I mean."

"Of course," she reluctantly agreed. "All I'm saying is I'd like to see the house knocked down or restored." She read Greg's face. "Look, we all die. If we're lucky we grow old before we do. You're the one who said he was old. So, he was one of the lucky ones."

"Always selling, aren't you? Putting a positive spin on death."

"That's what I do," Constance said, smiling and pulling herself into Greg's shoulder. "You said it yourself, I can sell anything."

Part 1

Chapter 1:

A few weeks passed. Sean sat in the corner of the tiny apartment. Wearing his current uniform of a faded t-shirt and gray boxer briefs, he quietly strummed his electric guitar, while the headphones transmitted the chords to his ears and blocked out any other sound. The lamp in the far corner provided the only illumination in the tiny room, and the lights of Jersey City (or Hoboken he was never quite sure) reflected off the Hudson River seventeen floors below. Two other guitars hung on the wall next to him, one acoustic, the other a vintage electric. He'd abandoned the amplification gear once the noise complaints began to pile up after they'd moved in. Some gear was stacked in the corner, the rest under the bed. They'd made the move from the spacious but "rustic" rental loft surrounded by other musicians in favor of this new construction high-rise for the sake of *creature comforts*, an *investment in their future* and for her sake, *privacy*. The fifty-thousand-dollar gift from her parents—in exchange for quietly eloping—provided the down payment. But they still had a crippling mortgage for 800 square feet "with a view." Their financial situation had become especially dire since Sean, at 29, hadn't worked in several months, and their savings was being quickly depleted.

Maya came through the front door without Sean noticing. She moved toward him and he was startled when she lifted the headphone cup from his left ear. He sat up straight, and seeing her, mumbled, "What the fuck?"

"Busy?" she asked. Dropping an envelope on the table in front of him, she said, "If you're going to be home all day, the least you could do is get the mail."

Recognizing her frustration, and feeling a little smug, he began lightly strumming again. The chords were barely audible through the headphones now sitting on his shoulders, "For the record, I cleaned the whole apartment today, and did the laundry."

"If cleaning this cracker box took you more than thirty minutes, you're doing it wrong. And you only do the laundry because you like playing with my panties."

Sean laughed, but kept strumming. "That I do. Although I prefer playing with them when you're wearing them."

Maya dropped her shoulder bag on the kitchen island and Sean asked, "So how was work? You're late, so I assume you either hit a stride or a wall."

"Both." As an artist—a starving artist—she had been working full time on her craft since her college days at NYU. But, she had yet to find her audience. As of now her effort was unpaid, so Sean's unemployment following his lucrative—if unfulfilling—marketing agency gig, was getting stressful. She sighed. "I'm trying out something new with the life forms. I'm experimenting painting on printed paper."

"What do you mean?" asked Sean. "Like wrapping paper?"

Maya had moved into the bedroom and was removing her outer layers of clothing intended to protect her from the chill of the early spring evening—and the creeps on the subway. Sean stood in the doorway, guitar still in hand. "No," she said. "Like printed pages from a book. I enjoy the interplay of the image against words. But now I think I want to try using a map as a background—like a nautical chart. See if I can get some naked, sailor vibe."

As Maya was unbuttoning her blouse, Sean set the guitar down and stepped up behind her wrapping his arms around her waist. He kissed her ear. "That sounds cool. I love how committed you are to your art. Your art will be adored, very soon, and you'll be famous." A moment later he added, "And we'll be rich." Maya turned around in his arms and reached hers up around his neck. Sean posed, "Maybe I could be your sailor," he quickly pulled his shirt over his head and stepped out of his underwear, "You've got your model right here. My rates are quite reasonable. I can get an anchor tattoo if it would help." Then he slid the blouse off of her shoulders, kissed down her neck to the shoulders. He unsnapped her bra to release her small breasts. She fell back onto the bed and he climbed on top to play with her panties again.

The next morning, Sean was in a chair with his feet up on the ottoman when Maya emerged from the bedroom pulling a V-neck shirt over her head.

"No bra today?" asked Sean.

"I couldn't find it," replied Maya. "I couldn't find any of them. Honestly, I thought having less space would make it harder to lose things." She pulled the ends of her long, dark hair from the crew neck, adding, "I don't really need it anyway." Maya was not normally dismissive of her body. She knew she had small breasts. But she also had the parts that mattered—below the waist and above the neck. And Sean didn't seem to mind. By all appearances, he was not a 'boob guy'.

As Maya poured herself a cup of coffee that Sean had made, Sean reached for his own cup from the side table. At that moment he noticed the envelope she'd dropped there the night before. He picked it up, looked at the return address and addressee—noticing the CERTIFIED stamp in green, then slid his finger under the flap.

"You got this out of the mailbox?" he asked.

"No, the concierge handed it to me. Why?" Maya sipped on her coffee and looked around the tiny kitchen for a donut or pastry, something to absorb the bitter brew.

"It's certified. Needed a signature is all. I'm surprised they didn't notify me when it came." Then Sean said, "Huh." Not as a question but still sounding puzzled.

"What is it?" she asked.

"Come here," he said. "Look at this."

She sat on the arm of the chair, took one side of the expensive, embossed stationery in her hand, pulling it toward her, while he held the other side not wanting to let it go.

"What?" she shouted, louder than necessary.

"Yeah, I don't know," he said, realizing they were thinking the same thing.

Maya noticed the clock and said, "I've got to run to catch my train. Call that attorney today and find out what it means."

"Could be the end to our money problems," he said, hopefully.

"Keep me posted." And she blew him a kiss as she grabbed her bag and jacket and ran out the door.

Chapter 2:

Greg returned from his six-mile run around the lake. Stepping through the double door of the master suite, he pulled off his yellow windbreaker to cool down. From the corner of his eye he spotted Constance dropping a brightly colored scarf into her designer travel satchel. Beyond her, the partially frozen lake he'd just circled twice was visible through leaded glass on the far side of the bed.

"It's warm for this early in March," he reported, breathlessly.

"Thanks for the weather report," she joked. Then adding, "After all these years, I just love it that the sight of me leaves you breathless."

"Always," he replied and moved toward her.

She rebuffed his attempt to embrace. "Not now, sweetie, you're all sweaty and this is silk," referring to her blouse.

"How long until your flight?" he asked.

"Oh, it's not until four, but I have calls to make before then."

He again moved toward her and grasped her wrists, leaning in to kiss her neck, while keeping his body a fair distance away from her precious blouse.

"Damn, you," she said.

"I'm going to take a shower," he mumbled against her neck. "Join me!. If you're going to be gone for two weeks, I think we both need this."

"You want me to let you fuck me and then start over with this look? Seriously, you think this just happens? Besides, you'll be joining me in New York next week, so it won't be that long."

He continued to nuzzle her neck, saying, "A week is too long for me. And you know I think you're gorgeous without any of this."

She pulled him into her and immediately felt his sweat wick into the silk. She felt his fingers working the pearl buttons down her back and the blouse fell forward from her shoulders exposing her lace bra. He pulled off his nylon tank top and let her fall back onto the king size down duvet. She gasped for a moment, as she always did when she saw his tight, young chest. She unzipped her slacks and slid them down along with her panties. She couldn't wait to have him inside of her. She whispered, "Fuck me, Greg!"

When they were done, she lay with her head tucked into his shoulder, her blonde bob in disarray. She looked over to her stained blouse on the chair, and said, "I don't know why I was so worried about that when there are nine more just like it in the closet."

"I'll remember that next time you resist," he joked. "I love you babe."

"I love you too, Greg." And then, sounding just the slightest bit desperate, added, "You know that, right?"

Greg held her tighter. She stayed entwined in his arms for a few minutes, remembering how they'd gotten to this moment.

It had been eleven years now since they met. She was only two years into her career in cosmetics sales. She had joined a network marketing company after her divorce to supplement her income as a local news reporter. It turned out she had a knack for it. She quickly left TV news to pursue this full time. She worked hard, traveled a lot, and made a very nice income—one she never would have seen in local news. She'd been burned in her divorce. He was her high school sweetheart, a high school football and baseball coach—which meant poor. He was accused of inappropriate touching of a player. Though nothing was proven, he was fired. It shattered her confidence. It took her a few years to decide to put herself back out in the dating world, when she was just a few years from forty. On a trip to California, she confessed her trepidation to one of her downline associates, which lead to a visit to a top cosmetic surgery clinic in Beverly Hills. On her first visit, she was assigned to an attractive, young technician to administer the Botox injections. His name was Greg. He was sweet, funny, and gentle. She had a hard time keeping her eyes closed during the procedure, despite the needle hovering just outside her field of view. She just wanted to look at the twinkle in his eyes and the beautiful smile that would peek through his well-groomed beard. She was disappointed when he said *all done*. He told her she could expect the results to last

24

for several months, but she made excuses to come back every few weeks for additional procedures. She knew he was happy to oblige, since every procedure put money in his pocket, but she was also becoming convinced he enjoyed seeing her too. Finally, before a scheduled procedure, she asked if there was any restriction on having a drink with a client. He said he didn't know and didn't care. He put down the syringe and agreed to meet her in Santa Monica that evening. They drank beer, snacked on fish tacos, walked along the boardwalk, and before the evening ended, checked into The Standard on the beach. After they made love the first time, she asked how old he was. He said, he was only a bit younger than her. Surprised, she asked how he knew her age. He reminded her he had access to her medical chart. She felt dumb for a moment, but he pulled her tighter to him and she realized it didn't matter to him. She couldn't believe it, but just like that, she was in love. They dated long distance for a while. She hated being away from him. Though he showed no signs of waning interest, she was constantly nervous she'd lose him to someone with more favorable proximity and age. Finally, on a planned visit to L.A., he picked her up in the new Jaguar sedan he'd bought himself, and drove her to the boardwalk where they'd spent their first evening together. With fingers so nervous they could never do an injection, he pulled a velvet box from the pocket of his perfectly fitted khakis and dropped to one knee to propose. She immediately said yes and was scared to death he'd drop the ring through the planks before it made it on her finger. There was no way it could have fallen through. The stone was larger than she ever imagined he could afford. Emerald cut, at least four carats, and just a hint of pink—her favorite color. A week later he quit his job, packed up his apartment, and joined her at her lake side mansion in her hometown, Minneapolis. That was ten years ago, a number she learned later was also their age difference.

"Hey," he nudged her from her thoughts. "You OK?"

"Just blissfully happy. I can't' wait to see you in New York next week."

"I'll be there," he said, as he moved to get out of the bed. "But right now, I've got to pee."

She watched and smiled as his bare butt cheeks bobbed back and forth as he made his way to the marble bath. She swung her own legs over until her feet hit the floor, bent over to locate her lace thong, pulling it on as she stood. She caught her image in the mirror. Not bad. A touchup to the hair and makeup, a fresh outfit, and she deemed herself suitable for flying.

A few minutes later, Greg emerged from the bathroom in a towel, having taken a quick shower. "Hey, can I drive you to the airport?"

"That would be nice," she affirmed. "I'll make my calls from the airline lounge."

He pulled on some jeans, commando as always. Then the blue cotton sweater that hugged his chest just the way she liked it. Then his driving mocs. He finger combed his wet hair out of his eyes, grabbed his keys and his leather jacket, saying, "Ready when you are."

She could only comment, "Ass." She always hated that guys like him could always look great with only five minutes of prep time. But then again, she wouldn't have her business without perpetuating the story that women need to work. . . and spend lots of money. . .to look their best.

Greg stopped the dark green Jag in the no parking zone outside of the Departures level at MSP. By the time he got to Constance's side of the car, she had already retrieved her carry-on bag from the rear seat. The March breeze had picked up and it felt like rain—hopefully no more snow. "I'll miss you," he said, reaching around for his goodbye hug.

"Me too," she said back. "It's going to be busy this week, but we'll have time to hang out when you get there next Tuesday. Stay out of trouble."

"You better make time for me," he joked.

"Only after I put you to work." She then pecked his lips.

"You can do better than that," he said and kissed her as deeply as a newlywed. Before he could release the kiss, a security officer urged them to wrap it up. They both laughed at the awkward timing. "Fly safe."

Constance gave him her usual wink, to say *I love you*, gracefully draped the bag on her shoulder and turned to walk into the terminal. As Greg watched her, the officer gave him another nudge to move while also complimenting his taste in cars. . .and women.

Chapter 3:

"Sean." Hardly waiting a second, "Sean," called out Maya as she burst through the front door. There was no sign of him. She made her way to the bedroom door, calling out again, "Sean."

He came out of the bathroom buttoning the waist of his jeans then zipping.

"Where have you been?" she asked.

"I had to pee."

"Not just now," she said, sounding irritated. "All day. Why didn't you call? Did you talk to the attorney?"

Sean walked toward her, buckling his belt. "I did," he said calmly. He sat on the edge of the bed while Maya stared him down.

"And," she commanded.

"Well," he was determined to draw this out to tease her. News like this couldn't be rushed. He noticed his phone in his back pocket, pulled it out realizing the battery was dead. "Damn, I forgot to charge it," he added.

She had guessed his phone was dead when she couldn't reach him all day. His mindlessness was one of her biggest peeves about him. "Sean, I've been waiting all day. I couldn't get any work done. What did he say?" She finally dropped the bag that had been resting on her shoulder to the floor.

"Do you want to sit?" he asked patting the area of the bed next to him.

She folded her arms across her chest and leaned against the doorframe a few feet away.

"I guess that's a no." He took a breath. "I called. I had to wait until ten, because they're an hour behind, you know." He got no response, so continued. "His secretary answered the phone."

"Assistant," she corrected.

"OK, assistant. She said he was in a meeting, but really wanted to talk to me, so she asked me to hold." He scratched his ear. "I was on hold for a long time." Then he added, as if he'd just realized it, "I guess that's why my phone is out of juice."

"Sean," she said, sounding more annoyed.

"Anyway, he finally picked up and we chatted. He asked me some background information about my folks. I guess he liked my answers, because then he told me that my grandfather had passed away recently."

"Grandfather?" she questioned.

"Yeah, news to me. I guess, just because I was adopted, doesn't mean there wasn't other family out there somewhere."

Maya moved over to the bed and sat down beside him. She leaned into his shoulder.

"Anyway," he continued. "It turns out that old granddad had some money. And assuming the DNA matches, it looks like I'm his only known heir."

"What?" she shouted, throwing her arms around him.

He raised his hands to temper her enthusiasm. "Hold on," he cautioned. "I never said he was *still* rich."

She sat back suddenly.

"He was. . .once. But I guess there's no money left. He blew through it somehow. But there is a house, in Minneapolis, that presumably will be mine."

"Wow," she said softly, in disbelief. After a second or two, questions flooded her brain. "How did the attorney find you? And you said DNA match?"

"Funny you should ask. Remember when we got those Ancestry kits thinking we'd see what our kids would look like? Well, I guess they tracked me through the database. They want to confirm the DNA though, so he sent me to some lab at NYU for another test. It's a chain-of-custody thing to confirm it's really me."

"You've already taken it?"

"Yeah, this afternoon. I stopped and had a beer with Gavin on the way back." He pointed to the bathroom, "That's why I had to pee."

She laughed at the pointless detail.

"Hey," he said. "I'm starving. You up for a burger? We can talk about this more then."

"Stella's?" she asked.

"Best burger downtown."

"OK," she said. "Let me grab my raincoat. It was starting to drizzle when I came in."

They made their way the four blocks toward the bar. The corner was dark, but the facade was well lit. Sean had stumbled upon it back when he was working as a bartender nearby. He walked in, alone and noticed it was crowded with women. He almost walked out, in no mood to be hit on. But this place had a different vibe, so he stayed. It was only after a couple of beers, when he and the owner behind the bar, Stella, started comparing tattoos that the rest of the room relaxed. He'd become a regular since then, since no one in here was looking for a straight man, or any man really.

"Hey, Stella," said Sean as they sat at the bar.

"Little Sean. How are ya tonight, hon?"

He said, "Great," and leaned across the bar to kiss her chubby cheek. "Blonde tonight," he said, referring to the curly wig on her head. "I like it."

"Nice contrast to my ebony skin, don't you think? Hey, I got some new ink."

"Cool," he said. "I can't wait to see it. You remember Maya."

"Of course." Putting her hand on Maya's, Stella said, "Hi ya, Missy."

Maya chose to assume that Stella always calling her Missy was referring to her marriage to Sean, rather than something derogatory. "Hi, Stella."

"Quiet night, tonight?" questioned Sean.

"It's early," replied Stella. "Thursday, so the music doesn't start til nine. The girls are all getting gussied up." She set two beers down in front of them. "The usual?"

Sean looked at Maya. Seeing her nod, he turned back. "You know it."

"Coming right up."

After she walked away, Maya continued with the questions that kept popping into her head. "When will you get confirmation on the DNA?"

"They said they'd be able to get it to Andy by tomorrow. Andy, that's the name of the attorney."

"Thanks, I figured that out." She took a sip. "Then what?"

"I guess he'll let me know if it's a match. But my head is already way ahead of that. I'm proceeding assuming it's a given."

"What do you know about the house?" she asked.

31

"Oh, here. Let me show you." He reached for his phone, forgetting it was sitting dead on the bed at home. "Damn. Do you have your phone?"

"Of course." She pulled it from the pocket of her coat handing it to him after unlocking it.

He typed on the screen. "I have the address." After a few seconds, he held the screen up for her. "Google street view."

"Huh," she said, judgingly. "Looks big."

He tapped the screen and held it up again. "Here's the satellite view. It does look big. Notice that there's a lake across the street." Sean paused to take a drink of his beer. "I don't know the details on it. I guess it's been in the family since it was built so there aren't any previous listings to check for information."

"Any idea of the value?"

"Nah. Andy didn't want to say. I looked up other listings in the area but without details it's hard to compare. It seems that a lot of the older houses around the lake are being torn down for new ones. So, it may just be the value of the land."

"It's got to be at least a million, don't you think?"

"Shit," he said. "Who knows what houses go for in Minneapolis."

Maya finished her beer just as Stella brought the burgers from the kitchen.

"Another?" asked Stella.

"Me too," confirmed Sean, holding up his half-empty mug.

Feeling a little tipsy, Maya leaned in to whisper to Sean. "I don't want to trash your dear departed grandfather."

"The grandfather I never knew existed?"

"Yeah, that one." She took a shallow breath. "His house . . .I guess our house. . .is really kind of ugly."

Sean burst out laughing. "Don't sugarcoat it my dear. Tell me what you really think."

Two more beers hit the bar.

"The burgers look awesome, Stella. When we're done with these, I want to see the new art."

Sean took a big bite of his sandwich. With his mouth full, and grease dripping down his chin, he mumbled, "Once the DNA is finalized, Andy says I need to go to Minnesota to meet with him, sign some papers and take possession."

"I assume you can turn right around and sell it at that point," said Maya.

"I guess," replied Sean.

"Good. The sooner the better." She held up her beer as if to toast. "Give my best to the heartland."

"I want you to come with me," said Sean.

"Oh, Sean. I don't have time for that," protested Maya.

"It's just for one night," he said.

"We'll fly in, take a look at the house, spend the night, and fly back."

"When are you thinking?"

"Next week. Maybe Friday. Fly back Saturday." His big brown eyes pleaded with her, "Please?"

"Maybe," she relented. "But then I'm going to the studio this weekend. And you can't be whiney about it."

"It's a deal." Turning toward the bar, he said, "Stella, one more beer for me."

Sean finished his burger. Maya made it through less than half.

"Missy couldn't finish?" said Stella.

This time it did sound condescending to Maya, but before she could say something back, Sean interrupted.

"So, Stella, let's see what you're sporting now."

Stella leaned over the bar, pulling down the front of her tank top. On her left breast, where the cleavage began, in a stylized font, surrounded by flowering vines it said Calvin.

"Calvin?" said Sean sounding surprised.

"My Wall Street hunk of man meat." Seeing the shock on his face, she added, "Just because I own a dyke bar doesn't mean I am one."

"Good point," replied Sean. "And good lesson. Never assume." Then to cut any lingering tension, he said. "I'm just disappointed I never made my move."

"Oh, hon, you know you couldn't handle this much woman." Realizing that some of her other patrons might be listening, she laughed before adding, "I got me a rich one with a big, um. . .well, you know. You stick with your Missy."

Sean winked. "Will do."

Maya was used to Stella being dismissive of her, but tonight she felt especially picked on. And Sean had said nothing. Angry, she headed for the door. Sean threw some cash on the counter and rushed to catch up with her.

When they opened the door, the rain was pouring down.

"Want to find a cab?" asked Sean.

"That will take forever in the rain," said Maya.

"Here then," he reached for his phone. "Damn, my phone. Hail a ride share on yours."

"No, let's just make a run for it."

The air had turned cold. He could see she was already shivering. He pulled off his puffer jacket and wrapped it around her raincoat.

"No, you'll freeze," she said, while pulling the jacket tight to her body.

34

"It's only a few blocks. If we're running, I'll be fine."

Less than fifteen minutes later they walked through the door of their condo. Both were dripping. Sean took the puffer jacket off of Maya's shoulders and dropped it into the sink in the kitchen. Her hair and her jeans were wet, but under her raincoat she'd stayed dry. Sean was soaked to the bone.

"I've got to get out of these," he said shivering badly. He disappeared into the bathroom.

Maya said nothing.

Twenty minutes later, Sean came back into the living room, saying, "I took a hot shower to warm up."

Maya was sitting in the modern chair in the window wearing an old thick, fleece hoodie. Her bare legs were tucked under her. She looked away from the window to see Sean standing with a towel around his waist while drying his hair with another. Forgetting her earlier anger, he smiled, appreciating his firm chest and the tattoos covering his shoulders and upper arms. He wasn't the smartest man she'd ever met, but he was sexy, and she knew he loved her. She'd married him over her parents' wishes, so she was committed to him—whatever that meant. She turned back to the window, knowing she loved him too.

Sean disappeared back into the bedroom and came back out a minute later wearing fresh underwear and a t-shirt. Noticing the glass in her hand, he said, "What are you drinking?"

"Scotch," she said quietly.

"Sounds good. I think I'll join you."

His own glass in hand, he perched on the ottoman in front of her. The rain cascaded down the wall of glass. "It's is still really coming down isn't it?"

She took a sip but didn't respond.

Sean reached forward to touch her knee. "Everything OK?" he asked.

"Just enjoying the view," she said. Both sat silently for a few moments. Maya turned to him. "This is where we're meant to be right now. Right here. It's just the way it should be."

"Of course," he responded.

She looked back to the window.

He stroked her knee. "Want to go to bed?"

"No, you go," she said. "I just want to sit here."

"I'll sit with you," he offered.

"No. You go to bed," she said sharply, sounding more insistent than she'd intended.

Chapter 4:

Greg stood naked in his walk-in closet staring at the wall of
shelves stacked with shirts and sweaters in a range of colors
and textures. On the adjacent rods hung jackets, slacks, jeans,
belts, and more shirts.

"What do you want me to wear?" he shouted to
Constance. He almost thought he heard an echo across the
cavernous room.

"Oh, you know I don't care," came the reply a few
moments later.

He did a silent eye roll, knowing that was far from the
truth. The last thing he felt like doing after the flight he'd had
from Minneapolis, was to have dinner with two of her work
associates, and their husbands, but such was life with
Constance in New York.

"Well what are you wearing?" he persisted.

"Too bad you can't just go like that," she said patting his
ass as she came into the closet in her long, satin robe. She
surveyed the shelves pulling a black cashmere turtleneck.
Then she reached for two hangers, one with tapered black
slacks and the other with a black/gray striped sport coat.

She turned to head back to her own closet.

"Shoes?"

She turned back selecting the Gucci loafers and black
socks patterned with silver horseshoes.

Handing the socks to him, she said, "It's chilly, so you'll
need socks. The horseshoes are for luck." When she was
halfway across the room, she added, "I'll be ready in fifteen."

"You look nice," said Constance when Greg walked into her closet in the prescribed outfit. "Will you zip me up?" she asked.

"New dress?" he asked. She had many in this shade of black, so he was never quite sure. This one, a sleeveless, modest V-neck with a gold zipper up the back.

"No," she said. Then slipping on the leopard print heels, "But the shoes are—and very expensive." At her dressing table she studied herself in the mirror and clasped a gold chain around her neck and bangle on her wrist. She already had the diamond studded gold hoops in her ears and ring on her finger. "Will you grab my coat?"

Greg opened a second closet. "Which one?" There were several color options along with the expensive furs that he had convinced her were no longer fashionable nor politically correct.

"What do you think? The camelhair?"

He it pulled from the hanger. When she was ready, he draped it on her shoulders. "Perfect," he said. "The driver is downstairs. Should we go?"

Constance dropped a lipstick in her black, satin clutch. "We should," she replied decisively, and with a smile.

There were a number of wealthy people, and more than a few celebrities who lived in their twin towered building, but Constance always felt as though she and Greg attracted more attention than most as they made their way through the lobby to their waiting car. They weren't high profile, so she imagined they were all asking themselves, "Who is this handsome couple?"

Besides two sales parties in their 22nd floor home, and two days for Constance in the corporate office, the rest of the week was time just for the two of them. They were regular visitors to the Met, Guggenheim and MoMA, as well as some smaller, upper east side galleries. They shopped on Fifth Avenue, dined at the trendiest restaurants, and even caught a performance of the newest Broadway musical. Greg ran in the park. While Constance was on calls, he'd read. And nearly every night, they made love. That was their magic. They just worked—physically. Whenever one might tire of being with the other—or they'd argue—sex would bring them back into harmony.

"It's been a fun week," he said, his arm under her neck as they laid in bed. The room was dark but was slowly growing brighter as the moon ascended on the horizon. "There's that moon again," he commented thinking back the roughly four weeks to Minneapolis.

"I wish you weren't leaving tomorrow," she said, wistfully.

"You can't keep the Oregon boy in the big city for too long," he joked. "I need my wide-open spaces."

"You've got Central Park across the street."

"Not the same thing, my dear. You could come back with me. This isn't your natural habitat either."

"Momma's gotta make money," she said without thinking.

She'd made that comment a few times before. He never liked it. It only served to highlight their age difference and sometimes make him feel like a kept man. He turned it back on her, saying, "I could go back to shooting up old ladies with Botox and you could work the cosmetics counter at Macy's."

Suddenly she sat up.

Realizing he'd struck too deep, he said, "Connie, I'm sorry. That was stupid thing for me to say."

She resisted his attempt to grasp her arm and got out of bed.

"Connie, come back to bed. I really am sorry."

"You go to sleep," she said. "I'm going to the other room to read for a while."

Greg laid in the bed and watched the moon rise for thirty minutes, thinking about his very comfortable life. She worked hard. But she loved it, so was it really work? All she asked of him was to love her and be arm candy once in a while to support her business. And he did love her, after all was said and done. She was his family. His only family. He got up from the bed to find her.

"What are you watching?" he asked, seeing her face illuminated by the TV screen in the den.

"Hitchcock," was her one-word answer.

"Suspenseful?" he asked, playing along with the one-word banter.

"Not when you're old and have seen it a hundred times."

There it was. He always underestimated her insecurity about their age difference. She took such incredible care of herself he didn't perceive the ten-year difference, or really any difference. But talking about it was not the solution. At least not right now.

"Mind if I join you?"

She moved the Vogue magazine and remote control to make space next to her on the sofa.

"Great. Can you pause it while I get movie snacks?"

She complied, hitting pause on the remote control. A few minutes later he returned with a bowl of fresh microwave popcorn and two glasses of chardonnay.

"That smells good," she said initiating the thaw.

40

Snuggling in next to her, he said, "Hit *play* when you're ready, my dear."

They made love the next morning. Back in harmony, he rode the elevator to the lobby and his flight from LaGuardia to Minneapolis.

Chapter 5:

Friday morning, Maya and Sean splurged on a livery car to Newark airport. Two hours after that, they were in the air and toasting each other with cheap airline champagne, and three hours later they were touching down at MSP. As they made their approach, both were surprised by the breadth of the city and the number of dots of water below. There were rivers and many, many lakes and ponds. The downtown area was very evident against the neighborhoods and parklands. In fact, there were two areas of tall, shiny buildings—Minneapolis and St. Paul they realized.

They had declined the offer of an airport pickup by the attorney Sean had been talking with. This was going to be a mini vacation after all. Their financial situation was no longer feeling so dire, and they wanted the freedom to explore. As they got in their rental car, Sean encouraged Maya to smell the air. The weather was a few degrees cooler than NYC, but the sun was strong and warm. Even Maya, from Connecticut, was surprised at the brightness of the blue Minnesota sky. They were scheduled to meet the attorney and a local real estate agent at the house at 2:30, so they plugged the address into the GPS hoping to find a cute spot for lunch on the way. The route took them through the Uptown neighborhood with local shops and restaurants. After a sandwich and recommended local favorite—wild rice soup (neither was a fan), they parked in front of the house a few minutes early.

"I guess that's it," he said, thinking back to the picture he'd printed.

"Looks a little rougher than I expected," she offered.

"The Google street view photo must have been taken a while ago. No wonder it's a tear-down. But it was probably quite stately in its day, don't you think?"

"No, I don't think so," Maya continued, "Connecticut has stately houses. Others along the parkway here are stately. This is just an ugly house." She stared at it for a few moments before continuing. "It's a gray box, or boxes actually. The windows are asymmetrical and a mix of styles. The lights, the balustrade, I guess it's trying to be, what? Italian? Mediterranean? It's a hot mess. And perfect for a Halloween haunted house."

"Yeah," was all he could say. "But it's our hot mess." Sean looked the other way, out the car window, toward the lake. "But look at this."

Maya turned, "Pretty. But it's not a view of the Hudson River, like we have."

"No, it's not," he agreed, in a tone that was unclear whether he saw that as a good or bad thing, but clearly feeling frustrated.

A Cadillac SUV pulled up behind them and a man and woman got out. As they walked toward the car, Sean and Maya got out as well.

Extending his hand, the attractive, middle aged attorney said, "Mr. Donaldson, I'm Andy Marshall."

"Nice to meet you, Mr. Marshall. But please, it's Sean."

"And Andy to you. This is my wife, Renee. She's a local real estate agent. She won't be able to represent you, should you decide to sell, but I asked her along to help with any initial market questions you might have."

"Nice to meet you . . . can I call you Renee?"

"Of course," she replied.

43

Before Sean could motion her forward, Maya stepped up to introduce herself. "And I'm Maya."

"Yes, the wife." Andy said.

"Partner," inserted Sean before Maya could. She hated being referred to as his wife, viewing it somehow as secondary. "And we will be selling."

Andy and Renee both shook her hand. "Fine," he said, taking a deep breath. "Shall we go in?"

Crossing from the street to the stairs leading up to the door, they paused at the sidewalk to let a runner pass by. Sean made eye contact with the runner, who nodded and said "thanks."

Sean said to the group, "Wow, friendly here. In New York he would have run me over."

Andy unlocked the massive oak door and swept his arm to offer entrance to the two-story foyer. Sean and Maya walked in. Renee followed immediately behind. Despite the bright midday sun outside, the interior was very dark. Sean noticed all the blinds were drawn—old fashioned, wood venetian blinds.

Seeing Sean look toward the windows for light, Andy volunteered, "The house has been sitting empty for a few weeks now. There's no security system so we've been keeping the blinds closed to guard against prying eyes. The bulk of the remaining contents have not been assessed and we're trying to discourage any break ins or thefts.

"Do the lights work?" asked Sean.

"Of course, forgive me," said Andy. "Renee, could you turn them on, please?"

Sean and Maya's eyes flew wide open when they saw the interior. Immediately Renee interjected, "As you can see the house went through a rather ill-conceived remodel in the 1970s. It's not that it was poorly done, it's just that, um, it wasn't a look that holds up over time."

"Is the whole house like this?" asked Sean.

"Luckily, no," said Renee. "They had a fire in this section of the house."

"Oh, no," said Maya.

Renee continued, "So it's the living room that you see here, the dining room back this way, and the kitchen in the rear of the house that all received the avocado and orange makeover. I'm sure it was very trendy in the moment. Unfortunately, between the fire and the remodel we lost most of the original features of the architectural design."

"What was that like?" asked Sean.

"Come this way," commanded Renee.

Sliding open, ceiling-high, double pocket doors, Renee revealed the original library. The overhead chandelier, once the switch was flipped, illuminated three walls lined with dark oak bookshelves. They were mostly empty now, but Maya could imagine them once filled with leather bound volumes as she'd seen in the homes of wealthy friends in Connecticut. A well-worn Chesterfield sofa sat under the window overlooking the lake they'd been eyeing earlier. Opposite the sofa was a massive desk, and on the wall, a large portrait of a gray-haired couple, a young man and a boy.

"I imagine the other side of the entry hall looked something like this once," concluded Renee.

Sean was staring at the painting. "Is this my family?" he asked.

Andy stepped up to the wall-sized artwork "Yes." Pointing to the older gentleman, he added, "Your great-grandfather, who built the house. Your grandfather, who died here last month." Then pointing to the young boy, "And according to the DNA match, this would have been your father."

Sean couldn't help himself, he reached up to the portrait and touched his father's face.

Maya said, "There's a strong resemblance, isn't there?"

Sean pulled his hand back quickly as if he'd done something wrong. "Sorry, I probably shouldn't be touching the art."

Andy chuckled, saying, "You own it. You can do whatever you like with it."

"What about the women? My Great-Grandmother and Grandmother?" asked Sean.

"I'm not sure," answered Andy. "There are scrapbooks and photo albums on the shelves. You may be able to find more information in them."

Sean made a mental note then looked at Maya for her reaction. She just grabbed his arm and asked Renee to see the rest of the house.

They spent most of an hour walking through the two floors and garden out back. As Renee had said, there was a large portion of the house that was mostly original. The wallpaper and curtains had clearly been updated through the years. And then there was the post-fire remodel. Paneling, shag carpet, crushed velvet upholstery. Sean and Maya agreed, it was probably *hip* at the time, but why hadn't it been updated since?

Renee pointed out some of the problems with the house. Spots on the ceilings likely indicating a leaky roof. Stucco on the exterior walls that was cracking and popping off. Broken windows. "You'd need to have an inspection," she said. "But you can probably count on lead paint and pipes. There's water damage but I haven't spotted any mold. The electrical system is certainly not up to code or proper load capacity. The hot water heating system is old but looks to be in good shape—and it's a very efficient heating method. But you don't have central air and really no easy way of installing it in an old home like this with plaster walls. Note the window air conditioners." She paused to make sure Sean and Maya were still listening. "It's too bad it wasn't maintained and updated over the years. I think it was a very well-built house—as they were back then when they had all the money in the world and no concept of pre-fab."

Seeing Sean wasn't going to ask, Maya broached the question she thought he should be thinking. "So, what's the market like for something like this?"

Sean was startled. He was still focused on the portrait in the library and his wife, *his partner* was skipping ahead to the money. Renee began to answer, but Sean cut her off, saying, "No, I don't want to go there yet."

Maya replied, "But Sean, you know that where this IS going."

He was slumped over. Feeling beaten down. "Dammit Maya, just let me absorb this for one minute!" he shouted.

There was quiet, before Andy finally spoke up. "Listen, Renee and I have to get going. You're spending the night in town, right? Why don't you two take some time to think and talk about things and questions you have. Look around some more if you like, and then we can reconnect tomorrow before you leave. I'll take whatever direction you give me."

Sean looked at Maya as if apologizing for what he knew was an outburst she'd been embarrassed by. "Yeah, Maya. Let's

47

go somewhere and talk so Andy and Renee can get on with their afternoon."

Andy held up the key, saying, you can look around some more if you like. Just turn off the lights and lockup."

Sean looked at Andy, confused.

Andy continued, "I have some papers for you to sign before you to take official possession, but they can wait. For all intents and purposes, it's your house now, Sean. You can stay and look around as long as you like."

Sean took the key, his posture even more slumped. Renee handed Maya her card. "Call me with any questions." Andy and Renee headed out the door.

Maya said, "I have to pee. Do you suppose the old man left any toilet paper in the place?" She disappeared to find a usable bathroom.

When she was done, she found Sean back in the library, looking at the portrait. "While I was sitting on the toilet, just now," she said, sounding flustered, "I saw a woman in the house next door staring at me. Creeped me out."

Sean didn't react. He just sat on the old sofa, staring at the faces on the wall. The resemblance to his dad was striking. He looked like a mischievous troublemaker. Sean could relate.

Maya had pulled a scrapbook off the shelf and began leafing through it. "Wow, she said. I've never been much into the family history thing."

"That's because you've always had one," Sean said hostilely.

"Let me finish," she said.

He looked at her wondering what she was going to say.

"As I was saying, I've never been much into the family history thing, because I didn't have many holes in mine. I grew up with parents and grandparents around. There were some stories that went back further than that, but I didn't need any more. But I can see why this would be a whole big new world for you. It just surprised me because you never seemed very curious about it."

"I wasn't, until now."

Yeah, I get it. So, we don't need to rush this. Well, I mean we do have to a little. We do have financial obligations . . . and no money."

"Just let me sleep on it," he said.

"Of course," she said, knowing she'd need to be more subtle in her coaxing. "Let's head to the hotel. I could use a drink and I'm sure you could too."

Sean nodded in agreement.

Before they left the library, Maya pointed to the scrapbook shelves, and asked, "Is there anything you want to bring back with you?"

Sean looked at the portrait, saying, "I'd like to bring this back."

Maya pulled out her cell phone, stepped back to frame the portrait properly and a flash filled the wall. Looking at her phone, she said, "There," and held it up for Sean to see.

"Thank you," he said with a smile and bent down to kiss her softly on the forehead.

"You're welcome. Now let's go drink."

Chapter 6:

By the time the taxi dropped Greg in front of their house, he was exhausted. The parties and other activities would be draining enough on their own, but the fight with Constance had wiped him out. In his classic manner of overthinking, he'd convinced himself on the flight that their fight was a result of his tiredness. Throughout the week, they'd been together almost constantly. That was rare. They were independent creatures, and both needed their space.

To clear his head, Greg dropped his bag on the bed and immediately changed into his running gear. After an energy bar, a guzzle of cold water, and a few minutes of stretching, he left through the back door.

He was only a few minutes into his run when he encountered the group on the sidewalk in front of the old, gray house on the hill. It reminded him of the night a few weeks back, when he believed he witnessed Mr. Miller's suicide. Oh, he was half a mile away, and had only seen to flash from the gun shot, but, after reading about it online, it hung with him like a bad dream. Made him shudder. He appreciated a distraction right now, so, as he trotted up the lake path, he started thinking about the group and how they may play into the future of the house and this neighborhood.

He noticed four of them. Two couples presumably—one young, the other ten or fifteen years older. The older couple was dressed professionally, for a Friday, and the younger had on nice, but casual clothing. Real estate agents, he wondered? But how could a young couple like that afford that house, even in its current state of disrepair. He hadn't seen it listed so wasn't sure about the price or the comps, but it was a prime piece of land and certainly expensive. Then again, maybe he's a tech guy. Or she is. Those kids seem to have ridiculous money.

As he came close to his first loop of the lake, he started watching to spot them again. The cars were still parked out front but no sign of the people. They were apparently still inside. But there was the chubby woman he'd seen around. He was pretty sure she lived in the colonial next door. He'd often wondered what her story was. She was sitting on the front steps, apparently on lookout. She didn't seem to notice Greg as he passed.

On his second loop, he had completed his six miles, so rather than run the extra two blocks to the gray house for another look, he headed up his front walk and around back to the door he'd left unlocked.

"Fuck, it's quiet," he said to no one but himself. Guzzling some more water, he headed up to the bedroom. He was going to take a shower but spotted the hot tub out back. Instead, he changed into swim trunks, stopped in the kitchen for a beer, and headed to the back patio. The pool was still far too cold for swimming, but they kept the Jacuzzi suitably heated all winter. As he sipped his beer, he worked to relax his muscles—shoulders, back, hip, leg. He cracked his neck. The bubbles filled his trunks with air. He wanted to strip them off, but, for a wealthy area of mansions, there was surprisingly little privacy from prying neighbors' eyes. "Such fucking problems," he said, chuckling to himself.

Back in his master bath, he opted for the delayed shower. It was nearly as satisfying as the soak had been but was missing the cold beer.

Feeling relaxed but no less tired, he headed to the kitchen where the maid had stacked the accumulated mail. He found nothing interesting in the pile, and certainly nothing that couldn't wait. In the refrigerator he found nothing of interest, nor fresh. He'd need to order some groceries. For now, he opted to order a pizza.

"Busy tonight?" he asked answering the door for the delivery driver.

"Yeah, we've been slammed," came the reply. "But Friday's there's usually an early rush, then it quiets down. Greg handed the driver a twenty for a tip on the twenty-five-dollar pizza he'd already paid for online. The cute college age student looked at him not sure if Greg was expecting change back.

"Keep it," said Greg, with a smile. "I was hungry, and I appreciate you getting here so fast."

"Thanks," the driver said. Then thinking back to the name on the label, he added, "Greg."

"And what's your name?"

"Dennis."

Greg reached out his right hand, holding the pizza in his left. "Nice to meet you Dennis."

Dennis held up the bill, saying, "I'd better get to my next delivery. Thanks again!"

"I hope to see you again," said Greg. "Have a good night."

The kid nodded. "You too. I'll keep an eye out for your next order," before turning to sprint to his old Civic at the curb.

Pizza in hand, Greg picked up the six-pack of beer from the kitchen and headed to the basement and his waiting man cave. Halfway down the steps it hit him. "Dennis thought I was hitting on him," he said out loud. He laughed, then added quietly to himself, "It's still fun to flirt."

Downstairs, his lair was exactly as he'd left it. Even the maid never entered. It wasn't that he had secrets or was hiding anything, it's just Constance had no interest in spending time in the basement and he didn't have any male friends. Or really any friends, or at least friends of his own.

The room wasn't large, but it fit the bill nicely. And he was proud of it, having built it himself with skills learned working construction in high school back in Oregon. To get to it, he had to cross the dark, musty, unfinished basement you'd expect in an eighty-year-old house. Inside there were two theatre style recliners and a large sofa covering most of the floor. An eighty-five-inch flat screen TV anchored one wall. Another wall was lined with bookcases holding hundreds of DVDs. The DVDs were nearly obsolete in the era of streaming video, but Greg found streaming services to be unreliable and inferior in quality to the Blu-ray library he'd assembled. The opposite wall had matching bookcases filled with books. Greg spent more time reading in this room than watching movies. These were the books, mostly mainstream crime dramas, that Constance deemed unsuitable for the shelves in the public rooms upstairs. The back wall was filled with the requisite framed movie posters. In the corner was a wet bar with refrigerator and microwave. Finally, next door was an updated bathroom with the basic equipment, as well as a shower and, his favorite, the sauna.

The room had one small, basement style window. An exhaust fan dominated the opening for when Greg wanted to smoke some weed. Constance didn't object to his occasional use but didn't want to risk it being detectable upstairs.

Five of the six beers went into the refrigerator, the sixth in the cupholder of his chair. The pizza box got its own chair. Cozy in his sweatpants and t-shirt, Greg took his seat and, with remote in hand fired up the massive TV and sound system. He'd start the evening with some things from Netflix he needed to catch up on.

For the rest of the evening and all of Saturday, Greg barely came out of his room. He drank all six beers the first night and ended up sleeping on the sofa. Saturday, he scrounged up a frozen bagel for breakfast before starting season one of Game of Thrones. Lunch was something else from the freezer and then more GOT. For dinner he ordered another pizza. Instead of Dennis, it was a pimply faced teenager at the door. *Just as well*, thought Greg, since he hadn't showered and was pretty sure he smelled and looked like shit.

With a hot pizza, fresh supply of beer from the kitchen, and yet another season of GOT queued up, Greg fired up the weed. He was pretty sure he'd never had pizza quite that good. And GOT was impossible to follow but *way more fun*. With hours more of GOT to play, Greg finally passed out on the sofa.

Sunday morning, when Greg woke up, the TV screen was black, and the exhaust fan was rattling in the window frame. *Fuck*, he thought as he sat up rubbing his eyes. He looked around the room before realizing he wasn't wearing his t-shirt anymore. He had vague recollection of a dream where Dennis had stopped by and they'd made out. At least he hoped it was just a dream.

"Enough," he said, acknowledging that his batteries were recharged, and the introvert could once again face people.

First stop was the shower. After, he headed upstairs, carrying his dirty clothes in front of him. Inside his closet he pulled jeans off the shelf and V-neck tee. He added Converse sneakers and a shawl collared cardigan, picked up his wallet and keys before heading out the door. As the garage door was opening, he took a long look at his face in the Jag's rearview mirror. Thank God he looked better than he felt. His eyes were a bit bloodshot, but the bags and dark circles were gone. He could use a haircut though. He shifted into reverse and was on his way. Coffee, a breakfast sandwich and the Sunday Times would help get him back on track.

He'd forgotten about the gray house until he came upon it. No visible activity. He wasn't sure what he expected. Maybe that was all a dream too. But then he saw the chubby woman. She was behind a bush, and he was pretty sure she was peeping in the window.

Chapter 7:

The hotel Sean had booked was in the heart of downtown, only a few miles from the house. He'd misread the GPS and ended up driving most of the parkway around the three connected lakes before heading back north. Maya seemed to enjoy the scenery for a while but grew impatient for a cocktail.

Sean's initial impulse upon entering the hotel room was to collapse on the bed. But Maya spotted the people on the sidewalk outside and dragged him out in search of a drink and some dinner. A small gallery caught her eye as they sought out food, and she made a mental note to stop back there after dinner. But by the time they returned, little more than an hour later, it was closed. A New York gallery would never close before eleven on a Friday night. It reminded her, that all of this downtown was nothing more than a quaint Manhattan neighborhood. All the foot traffic was gone too, with office workers having retreated to their suburban homes. She was anxious to get back to work. Back to her studio.

They were both exhausted when they got back to the room. Hotel sex, which was a hallmark of their travels wouldn't be happening tonight. Maya slept soundly, knowing she was headed home tomorrow and soon the financial troubles that had been worrying her would be over. Then Sean would get a job and she could focus on her art. Sean didn't sleep at all.

As daylight filled the room, Sean felt a hand reach around to his stomach. Then Maya pulled herself into his back. Her hand was like ice and bare nipples rock hard against his skin.

She naturally ran cold, but this was extreme, even for her. "Warm me up," she whispered in his ear.

Without moving, he put his hand over hers. "I want to stay," he said.

She immediately recoiled.

"Wait," he begged. "Let me explain."

"There's nothing to explain. We're getting on that plane this afternoon and going home—where we're from. Where we live. Where we're going to continue to live. We're New Yorkers!"

"Just for another day or two," he said. "I want to go through the scrapbooks and photo albums."

"Pack them up and ship them back," she suggested bluntly.

"It's not the same he said. This house has been in this family for generations. I just want to experience it. I feel like the house was saying something to me. Like my granddad was talking to me."

She spun around, facing him on her knees. "Seriously?" She grabbed his hands and was about to speak again, when her phone buzzed on the nightstand. She leaned over to look at the caller ID. Maya sprang from the bed, picking up the phone in the process. She went over to the window. Sean stared at her silhouette against the bright background of sky. Despite her long hair and thong panties, with no makeup and a flat chest she looked oddly boyish.

"Hi, Todd," she said excitedly. "Why are you calling? What's going on?"

Next she shrieked. Sean could tell it was excitement but for a moment he hoped it didn't bring a call from the front desk.

57

"That's amazing. When?" She was now looking at Sean who was clearly not tracking. "I'll be back tonight. Yeah, bye."

Her mood was instantly changed. A huge smile came across her face.

"What is it?" he asked.

"That was Todd."

Sean nodded since that had already been established.

"The three of us, the studio partners, have been invited to submit pieces, for a gallery crawl in early May." She jumped on the bed then off, standing for a moment trying to decide what she needed to do first. "I have to get back to New York," she said. She looked into her bag, still not knowing what she was doing. She put her hands to her head to collect her thoughts. "I need to shower."

"So, you're OK if I stay for a day or two?"

"I don't give a shit what you do, Sean. But see if you can get me on an earlier flight out of here." She disappeared into the bathroom with her bag, and uncustomarily, shut the door.

Fifteen minutes later, she came out of the bathroom, fully clothed in jeans and a light sweater, no bra. Her hair was still wet, but she didn't care.

"I was able to move you up to noon flight," he said.

"Great. What time is it now?"

"Nine-forty-five. You have plenty of time. Let me throw on my jeans and I'll drive you," he offered.

"No." She came over to him still sitting on the bed in only his gray underwear. "I'll take the hotel shuttle. You just take care of whatever it is you have to do as quickly as possible. I need you back home." She put her hands on the side of his face and kissed him. Next she was up, grabbing her bag and jacket. Before she walked out of the door, she said, "And don't spend any money we don't have yet!"

"You either," he called back to her.

Sean got up and walked to the window. Looking to the southwest he wondered if he could figure out where his house might be on the horizon.

: : :

Monday night, Maya came home from the studio to find Sean. He hadn't told her he was coming. He had two large suitcases packed, along with his guitar and some audio equipment.

Her first words were, "You're home." Her eyes narrowed as she looked at the piles, "What's going on?"

"He crossed to her and took her hands. "I wanted to tell you this in person."

"What's going on, Sean? You're making me nervous. Are you leaving me?"

"Relax," he began.

"Fuck relax," she blurted.

"Maya, shhh. I've got an idea." She didn't interrupt so he continued. "I'm not done with the house. I know we're not going to keep it, but I want to spend some more time with it. I talked with Andy and Renee and I think I can rehab the house and then flip it. That way I can spend more time with the house and in the end my history doesn't get torn down."

She just stared at him. He waited. Finally, she said, "What the fuck do you know about rehabbing a house? And where are you going to get the money? Just sell it with the stipulation it can't be torn down, like they did with Grey Gardens."

"If this house had a Kennedy connection, that might work. But it's just the Minnesota Millers. Seriously, I used to help my dad around the house when I was younger. There are books and YouTube videos. I'll figure it out."

"And the money?" she was daring him to say what she feared.

"I spoke with an agent and there's a lot of interest in this building. If we sold now, we'd walk away with a couple hundred thousand—between the down payment and the appreciation."

"You're not selling our home!" she shouted.

"We can't pay the mortgage," he said. "We're already behind. Unless you want to get a job."

"Fuck you, Sean. Fuck you! You get a job! We had a nice life until you got yourself fired."

"Calm down," he said knowing it was the wrong thing to say.

"I will not calm down," she shouted louder. "Where am I supposed to live while you're playing Mr. Fixit?"

"With the money we get, we could rent a little place for you, maybe closer to the studio," he suggested.

"And you've decided all this without even talking to me about it?"

"I just wanted to see if the pieces would even fit before I brought it up. And it seems to . . . if you're agreeable."

He let her sulk for at least a minute before he finally said, "Come on Maya. What do we have to lose?"

He reached for her and she allowed herself to be enveloped in his arms. He held her tight, but she didn't return the hug.

He could feel she was sobbing into his chest. "Do you want a divorce?" she asked.

"God no!" he protested. "I want you to come visit as often as you can. Maybe you can paint a fresco on the ceiling of our new living room." He pushed her away from him to look into her face, still holding fast to her arms. "And I'll come back here often too. I'll definitely be back in May for your art crawl. And every other exhibit you have. I love you."

She wiped her eyes and then her nose.

"OK?" he asked.

She reluctantly nodded her head and wiped her nose again. "So, what's the plan?"

"I know you're busy with your work, so I'll take care of everything. I'll get the condo listed. You just need to keep it tidy for showings—which shouldn't be hard without me here. And we'll take it from there."

"And are you staying in the house?"

"Yeah. There's lots of room so I can set up camp in a room or two and work around it. I spent last night there. The beds are a little lumpy, and there are some strange noises . . . which is probably true of any old house."

"Maybe it's haunted," she said finding her humor again.

"Could be," he agreed. "Besides granddad killing himself there, it appears his first wife died there too. In the fire that precipitated the remodel. Which, by-the-way, was orchestrated by his second wife."

"What, which did she orchestrate? The death or the remodel?"

"Maybe both," he replied. "There's some weird history there."

Maya emitted a small laugh and he knew he'd won her over. He kissed her forehead and she didn't know whether to feel loved or manipulated.

"I'm not flying back until tomorrow. Can I show you in there," motioning toward the bedroom, "how much I appreciate your support?"

"You'd better," she said defiantly, before embracing him.

His arm went up her back. Still no bra. "Still all lost?" he asked.

"Maybe they'll turn up when I pack." she said.

He kissed her in his arms, saying, "Thanks for being a good sport."

Chapter 8:

Sean had been living in the house for a little more than a week with little to show for it but working Wi-Fi and a couple dozen 'how-to-rehab' YouTube videos under his belt. In the meantime, he'd also managed to stock the avocado green refrigerator and liquor cabinet. He'd eyed the old man's wine cellar but resisted, hoping something in there might have sellable value.

During the day, Sean would wander the house surveying the needed work then sit in front of his computer to watch the corresponding videos. He'd also, occasionally watch episodes of This Old House for motivation. In the evening he'd pour through the scrap books and photo albums. What, to the family, was probably a carefully curated family history, to an outsider made little sense. And there was surprisingly little on the internet to help connect the dots.

Sunday evening, just after sunset and a microwaved burrito, Sean settled onto the sofa in the library with a scotch and collection of high school yearbooks. Only a couple of sips into the first folio, he heard a rapping on the front door, followed but a "Hello?" The day had been warm, so the door was open with only the screen door as a buffer. Startled, Sean jumped from the sofa to investigate.

As he approached the door, Sean flipped on the porch light. Standing on the other side of the screen was an unfamiliar woman, maybe in her late fifties. She was heavy, with shoulder length blonde hair and an engaging smile.

"Hi," she said. "Are you Sean?"

"Yeah," he answered. "How did you . . ."

Before he could finish his question, she volunteered. "I'm Katie Jo. I live next door."

Now he knew who she was, but it still didn't explain how she knew his name.

"I brought you some cookies," she continued.

He opened the screen. "Would you like to come in?" he invited.

"Just for a minute, if I may."

Once in the entry hall, he took the plate of cookies from her. "Thank you. They look great."

"Almond," she offered. "One of your granddad's favorites."

"Let's go in here," he said, pointing toward the library. Once in the room, he asked, "Can I get you a drink?"

"Oh, no," she said. I can't stay. "I just wanted to introduce myself and welcome you to the block."

Sean sat back down on the sofa and pointed to the neighboring chair. She perched on the edge of it as if she might want to leave quickly.

He set the plate on the coffee table and picked up his glass. "Have you lived here long?"

"Oh my," she said. "Pretty much my whole life. I grew up in that house. I went away to college then got married. About the time that fell apart, my mother got sick, so I moved back to take care of her."

"Oh, I'm sorry to hear about your mother," said Sean.

"Don't be," said Katie Jo with a laugh. "The old broad is still kicking over there. Pretty sure she's hanging on just to get back at me for all the trouble I caused her when I was young."

"A real wild child, huh?" Sean joked, lifting his glass in a toast. "You never said, how did you know my name?"

"The neighbors. . .well, we like to keep tabs on what's going on."

"Like a neighborhood watch?"

"Essentially, yeah."

"So, if you've lived here so long . . ."

"Watch it," she interrupted. "You're making me sound old."

He laughed. "Not my intention. But, did you know Mr. Miller well?"

"Of course. I knew all the Millers." She looked at the painting. "Your dad was a year younger than me, but we hung out together in grade school and high school. We used to play hide-and-seek in your granddad's department store, downtown. And when we were old enough, he gave us jobs in the store."

"Does the store still exist?" asked Sean.

"Sadly, no," answered Katie Jo. "He had a number of stores by the end, but then he sold them to another brand. Industry consolidation, you know. The death of retail. He was smart and sold at the right time."

"You know I've been going through the family scrap books and photo albums and I have so many questions. Maybe you could fill some of the blanks."

"Of course," she replied. "I'd be happy to. But I need to get back to mother or she'll be in a real fit. Some other time though." She stood. "Enjoy the cookies."

"Thank you again," he said. "I'm sure I will."

"And I'll pick up the plate in a few days." She opened the screen and walked out, letting its spring slam it closed. Turning back, she said, "Bye," with a little wave. Rather than

65

going down the steps to the main sidewalk, she trotted across the grass to the neighboring yard.

He blamed it on the cool air that had invaded the darkness when he closed the heavy oak door over the screen, but he wasn't looking for any more unannounced visitors tonight. Sean refilled his cocktail and returned to the sofa, lifting the cellophane and retrieving a cookie on the way. Paired with the scotch, it was surprisingly good. He had a second and a third of both.

∷ ∷ ∷

Greg had passed the gray house twice a day on his runs for nearly two weeks and not seen any activity. He was ready to dismiss the idea that the young couple might be moving in when he rounded the corner and spotted someone. At the curb was a young man, maybe half the couple, leaning against a car, staring up at the house. A vente Starbucks cup went up to his lips and back down again. Greg thought about stopping to strategize what to say—how to start a conversation. But this wasn't a meet-cute, so he kept running until he got close enough to confirm it was the guy. He stopped a few feet short, confident he was in the guy's peripheral vision. Greg looked up at the house, then back to the guy.

Greg took the last two steps. When the guy turned to him, Greg asked, "Thinking about buying it?"

The guy looked back up at the house, pointed to it with his coffee cup, and answered solemnly, "I already own it. Now I'm trying to figure out what to do with it."

"No shit," replied Greg. "Congratulations." He reached out his hand, "I'm Greg, by the way. I live a couple blocks further up the road here. I saw you when you were here before."

Sean accepted the handshake, saying, "Thanks. Yeah, I remember. I'm Sean."

Sean wasn't quite sure what to make of the neighbor situation. Two, in as many days, stopping to say *hi*. After more than a year he had yet to have a conversation with anyone in his NYC building. He continued to stare at his house.

Standing there, a bit too long, was beginning to feel awkward, and he was just about to move on, when Sean asked, "You lived around here long?"

"Yeah. Almost ten years. My wife has had the house longer. I moved in after we met in L.A." Greg wasn't sure why he had volunteered information that hadn't been asked. Then he reminded himself, that's how conversations worked.

"L.A., huh? Cool. I'm from New York."

"My wife and I have a place in New York too. That's where she is now. I'm flying out this afternoon."

Sean didn't reply for a minute. Greg watched him continue to stare up the hill. Once again, he was just about to say his goodbye, when Sean spoke up.

"Have you seen the inside before?" Sean gestured toward the house with his cup.

"No, I haven't," replied Greg. "I only met Mr. Miller once. Out here on the sidewalk. I think that was the only time I saw him. He had to come down the steps to get his newspaper that hadn't been tossed properly. He was pissed." Greg laughed, happy to provide a little color on the past owner.

"He was my grandfather," said Sean, dryly.

"Oh, no," said Greg, feeling his face flush. "I'm so

sorry about his passing."

"I never met him," added Sean. He stood up from his leaning stance, adding, "Would you like to see inside? Maybe you've got some ideas for me."

Greg was conscious of the time. He had a flight to catch. But he was intrigued, so he said, "Yeah, I would."

The house was stuffy inside. Greg removed his windbreaker and Sean his sweatshirt. Both wore tank tops. Greg noticed the lean torso and tattoos on Sean's arms. Greg had no tattoos himself. Constance wasn't a fan of them, and he thought maybe now he was too old anyway. But they did look sexy on Sean. Greg wondered if there was any meaning behind the design. Sean saw that, other than the age difference, and the height—Sean was an inch or two taller, he and Greg had similar physiques.

Sean turned his attention to the house, guiding Greg through room by room. Greg hadn't known what to expect. This house was always somewhat of an anomaly on the block. Through various neighborhood meetups he'd learned a little of the history. He knew it had been in the same family since it was built. There had been a fire at one point, and someone died. There were other houses on the lake that had long-time, elderly residents and hadn't been kept up to date, but this one was definitely in the worst repair.

The rooms on the main floor were to be expected. They lingered in the library so Greg could get a good look at the portrait. He agreed the young boy resembled Sean, and even himself in early photos—but then all kids look alike. Satisfied, they crossed the entry hall. Greg couldn't help but laugh out loud at the seventies update. "What were they thinking?" he said. "To be honest, I kind of like the retro feel of it, but not in this house."

On the second floor, there were multiple bedrooms and bathrooms. Greg lost count. At the end of the hall was the bedroom Sean had taken over as his own. It wasn't the master. Greg wondered about that then realized Sean was probably trying to stay out of the way of the work. Not that any work was underway. The room had a double mattress on a Queen Ann frame. Sean hadn't made the bed, which also made Greg smile.

"Good to see you found a room to sleep in," said Greg.

Sean had more or less forgotten about the bed. "I tried it up here, but I've taken to sleeping on the couch in the library." Greg thought about all the times he slept on the basement couch.

Next door was a sitting room, with a guitar, electric keyboard, an amplifier and some speakers. "Well, are you using this room? Are you a musician?"

"Frustrated musician, slash producer," responded Sean. "And yeah, I like to play but realized early on I'd never make any money at it, so I went the corporate route instead." Then feeling the need to explain the large speakers, he added, "I couldn't use any amplification in our New York condo, obviously, so it's been fun to crank things up here a little."

When they finished the second floor, Sean said, "That's it."

"Can I see the basement?" asked Greg. "I studied architecture. I love all the surface details, like moldings, but the foundation is where the real truth lies."

"Uh, OK," agreed Sean. "I've only been down there a couple of times myself."

As they descended the old wooden steps, Sean pulled the cord that turned on the ceiling fixtures and light flooded the space. It was the full footprint of the first floor. Posts and beams but no walls from one end to the other. The foundation walls were stone. The floor was dry, owing to its perch on the hill.

"Nice," said Greg. Then he noticed something at the far end of the room. He walked closer and when the image became clearer, he jumped back startled. Bodies upon bodies. Some standing, some laying down, some cut in half. But all had their eyes open. It took a moment before he realized what he was seeing. Mannequins. Dozens of mannequins.

Sean laughed, "Yeah, that was my reaction too. Still gives me nightmares."

"You could have warned me," chided Greg.

"Now what's the fun in that?" answered Sean. "And just so you know, I don't think old Carl Miller was a perv. I assume these came from his stores. Look how old they are."

"Still, having a bunch of naked mannequins in your basement does seem rather pervy." Sean nodded in relative agreement to Greg. "What's in the attic," joked Greg. "More bodies?"

"You might say that. Decades worth of old Time magazines and Playboy," answered Sean seriously.

"Those might be worth something," said Greg.

"Which?" asked Sean.

"Both. That is if the centerfolds aren't all crusted up."

"Eww," said Sean disgusted. "He was an old man."

"Not always," corrected Greg. "And don't underestimate us old guys. We can be as horny as anyone."

70

It was cool in the basement and Sean suddenly felt a chill, "Let's go back upstairs now."

"Sure," agreed Greg.

Back on the first floor, Greg wandered into the living room. He wanted to bask in the seventies flashback. It was before his time but still familiar from reruns of old sitcoms he'd watched on TV as a child. He sat on one of the two large sofas that anchored the room. The velvet felt soothing on his bare legs. Sean sat down opposite him. "Well?"

"In my opinion, it's a very solid house. Oh, it's got plenty wrong with it. It's an awfully big job for one person to take on, especially with no experience. Let me ask you this, what do you want to end up with when you're done?

That's when Sean lost it. As if a damn burst, Sean immediately responded, "I have no fucking idea. I've been wandering around here for nine days and I have no idea what to do. I inherited this piece of shit house. I should have just sold it, but instead decided I needed to bond with it, and fix it up. But I don't know what the fuck I'm doing. I don't even know where to start."

Leaning into Sean, Greg quietly said, "You can hire people for that, you know."

Fuck, I don't have any money for that. My wife was right. I'm making her sell our condo in New York to chase after something. I fucked this up so bad!"

"Hey, hey, hey. Relax. It's overwhelming. I get it," consoled Greg. "But there are always options. You can look into grants and loans. Maybe the historical society has some funds for restoration. It's worth a lot—the property alone. You're sitting on a financial windfall."

Sean had calmed down. He wiped the tears from his face.

Greg continued. "Don't worry about the money right now. What's your vision for this place?"

Sean started to look around the room as if formulating his ideas.

Greg looked at his Apple watch, saying, "Listen, I really have to leave if I'm going to catch my plane. But when I get back, I can help."

"Why?" asked Sean.

"I've got time on my hands. I work in real estate. I had a construction job in high school, and I like this kind of shit. This house been a blight on the neighborhood for years, but I think it has potential. And I'd rather see it fixed up, brought into the twenty-first century than replaced with another one of these modern behemoths that are being built."

"You better not be fucking with me," said Sean wiping his nose.

"I think you'll find I'm pretty reliable," laughed Greg. "I really have to go. I'm due back here next Sunday, but here's what I'd like you to do in the meantime. Talk to your wife to make sure you're on the same page. Then document, on paper or your computer, as much detail as you can. Budget—how much can you afford to spend? Timeline—how long do you have before you need to see to payback? Vision—given time and money, what would you like to end up with? Then start thinking about the plan. I can help with that, when I get back, if you like. OK?"

"Who are you?" asked Sean with a smirk.

"Your best friend or worst enemy. . .but probably something in between," answered Greg. Time will tell I guess."

"OK," agreed Sean.

"Hey, what's your number? When I get to the airport, I'll text you some details. You can Google the shit out of me. But you'll find a lot more on my wife."

Sean gave Greg his number. Then said, "Thanks. Sorry for the outburst."

"Hey, no worries. I've got to run." Greg reached out his hand to shake Sean's.

Sean took Greg's hand and pulled him into a hug. It lasted longer than he realized, but he was grateful to finally have some support. . .even from a relative stranger.

Chapter 9:

Constance called for the champagne to stop flowing at nine. This was her standard signal to guests that the party was ending, and it was time for them to conclude their orders and make their way home. It was a trick her mentor had taught her. The woman who brought her into the business. Vivian had taught her several things: Always use your full name in business—it commands respect; Never forget what role you're playing at any moment—seller, boss, wife; Hold onto your husband whatever it takes—it's too hard to train a new one, and you can seek companionship elsewhere, if needed. Constance was a believer, though she had never needed *other* companionship.

"Connie, I'm so disappointed we didn't get to see Greg tonight," commented one guest.

"It's Constance," she said firmly. In this context she was always Constance. "Yes, it's too bad. His flight was delayed due to the weather." If he had made it in time, there would have been a strategically timed return from a run or the gym, so the ladies could see Greg, muscled up and sweaty. She liked to think of it as "aspirational marketing." Liberal use of these products could get them a young stud too. She and Greg both laughed about it. She worked so hard to build and maintain her business, he never minded helping.

When the last of the guests left, Constance retired to the massive master bedroom, leaving the catering staff to finish cleaning. She was annoyed she hadn't heard from Greg since the text telling her his flight was delayed. But he should have been here two hours ago.

By the time Greg arrived, a little after eleven, she was in bed. She wore his favorite black nightgown, low cut and lace, but had no intention of rewarding him tonight. She paged through her Vogue while the rain tapped against the windows. She dozed off and didn't hear him come in.

"You look beautiful," he said.

"And you look soaked," she replied in a haze.

"Yeah, it's been one fucked up night. First the flight was delayed in Minneapolis because of thunderstorms. We finally get in the air, it's bumpy as hell for the first hour. We finally hit calm air, then it got bumpy again and we had to circle LaGuardia for an hour waiting for a break in the storm here. I finally got a cab and he can't get close to the building. They're working on the facade of the old building across the street. . . *in the rain. . .*and have the street closed. I had to walk the last two blocks."

She knew he was looking for sympathy, but she wasn't eager to give it. "You should have flown in yesterday, like I asked."

"Coulda, shoulda," he agreed. "I've just never had it been this bad before—on both ends."

"Why didn't you text me from the plane. . .or when you landed?"

Greg pulled the wet phone from his back pocket and tossed it on the bed. "I think I need a new phone. The battery won't hold a charge."

Constance was holding firm on her resolve to make him feel bad about missing her party. That resolve lasted until he stripped off his wet shirt. Seeing his bare shoulders and chest, she melted. She knew it. She was addicted to him.

"Here, let me get you a towel," she offered, as she finally rose from the bed.

By the time she came back from the bathroom with the thick towel, he was naked. She wrapped the towel around his shoulders, saying, "You must be freezing."

"Nothing a stiff scotch can't fix." He grabbed the towel and began drying himself.

Constance retreated to the bathroom again. When she returned, she was wearing a fluffy terrycloth robe and carrying another for him.

"Here, put this on," she said. "Let's get you that drink."

"Is there any food left over? I'm starving."

"Let's see," she said.

They made their way to the kitchen and Constance flipped on the lights. The room was ultra-modern, well equipped, and many of the appliances had never been used. The space was mainly for caterers to arrange platters to be passed at one of her parties. Constance could cook but preferred to do it at the home in Minneapolis where they lived. New York was where she worked. She opened the refrigerator to survey the contents while Greg poured himself a drink.

"Want one?" he asked, holding up the bottle of scotch.

"Sure," she said. "Make it light."

He added water to her glass, on top of the ice.

"Pickings are slim," she said. "Want me to order a pizza? Or anything? I'm sure we can have something sent up from the hotel downstairs."

"A cheeseburger would be great," he said, digging in a cupboard and finding a box of crackers.

A few minutes later, she said, "Done. Fifteen to twenty minutes."

Constance sat on the stool at the island, next to Greg. He put his hand on top of hers, saying, "Thanks. And I'm really sorry for being late and missing the party. I know this was an important one."

She looked out the window at the rain. "Some things can't be helped."

He looked out the window too. Through the rain streaked window, the park across the way was mostly dark. They sat in silence until he leaned in, saying, "I love you."

He kissed her for the first time in more than a week.

"And I love you, Greg," she said when their lips parted. They might have retreated to the bedroom at that moment, but the doorbell rang.

"Food is here," he said. "I'll get it."

When he returned to the kitchen, Constance was opening a bottle of Pinot Noir. Greg was ready to open the box, when she said, against all her own rules, "I've got an easy morning tomorrow, let's watch a movie and eat in bed."

He grinned and said, "I don't think I could love you any more than I do right now."

The next morning, they slept until the sun made its way around the east side buildings. He looked at the clock. It said nine.

"Fuck," he said.

"Not the way I feel," replied Constance, in her reliable wit. "What time is it? I don't want to open my eyes."

"Nine," he answered.

"Fuck," she said.

"You just said 'No'," he joked.

"Not funny, Greg."

"I'll go make some coffee," he said sitting up, still wearing his robe.

"Please," she said, grateful he offered first.

"We must have fallen asleep mid movie. It's on standby. Want it on or off?"

"Off," she directed. "And coffee. Please!" She was still in her robe as well.

He clicked the remote and the screen went black before the unit lowered itself into the cabinet.

"Be right back," he said.

"And take the boxes, bottle, and glasses. It smells in here."

His head wasn't in the mood, but he still had to laugh as he picked up the remnants of last night.

Constance used the bathroom, then crawled back in bed. Even with her thick robe, she was chilled and pulled the covers over her, resting her head on the pillow.

Greg came back with a tray. Two cups, an insulated carafe filled with coffee, four slices of lightly buttered toast, and two aspirin.

"You're my prince," she said swallowing the pills with her first sip of coffee.

He took a sip himself, and said, "Tell me about your week."

She leaned back against the pillow, "Well," she began. It wasn't all about her own sales effort. As a top producer, the company paid her a significant salary to coach and mentor other sales associates. She spent her days in one-on-one phone calls, conference calls, and attending parties hosted by new associates. Finally, she took a big gulp of coffee and said, "Enough. Enough about my boring work. I want to hear about you."

"Your work isn't boring. You love it." He crawled to the foot of the bed, reclining opposite her. "Well, I had an interesting morning, yesterday. I met a cute guy."

She suddenly straightened up, nearly pulling her foot from his hands. That wasn't the kind of thing she expected her husband to say. "Tell me more," she said cautiously, remembering the past he had told her about.

"No, I don't mean cute physically. Although, I guess he's pretty good looking. I mean cute as in clueless."

She relaxed a bit.

Greg continued. "Remember the gray house on the hill a couple blocks south of ours on the lake?"

She stared blankly.

"We drove past it a few weeks ago. There were police and EMTs out front."

"Not really," she admitted.

He grabbed his phone off the table and pulled up a picture he'd taken. "Here. This one."

"Oh, the eyesore."

"Well, it's pretty run down. The old guy that lived there died a few weeks ago and this kid and his wife inherited it. He's the grandson I guess, although there's more to the story that he didn't tell me—not yet. Anyway, this kid, he's probably around thirty."

"If he's a kid, what does that make me?"

Greg ignored her comment. "Anyway, he seems to think he's going to rehab it himself. But he doesn't have a clue what he's doing."

"With all the tear-downs that have been happening lately," she said. "I would think this would be a candidate for that."

79

Greg laughed. "Yeah, I've heard you say the same thing about some of your clients before gussying them up with your products."

Constance rolled her eyes, not appreciating the comparison to her livelihood or the choice of the word *gussying*.

"Anyway," continued Greg. "I thought the same thing about this house, but he says he wants to bond with it and preserve his family history."

"Good for him," said Constance half-heartedly.

"Sure. If he had any idea what he was doing. Or had the money to pay someone else to do it. He has neither."

She grabbed his foot to massage it. He initially pulled away, ticklish. "So, there's more to this story, right? I sense you're now somehow involved. And *no*, we can't afford to invest in his boondoggle."

"Oh, God no," he said. "I wasn't thinking that at all." Although he would have assumed *affording it* was not the issue. "But I do want to help."

"Then what does helping look like?"

"Initially, I guess, it's using my architecture and real estate know-how to advise what he can do with it. It's one thing if he was going to live there but he's planning on selling it when he's done. He's from New York and his wife is still here." Greg thought about the similarity to himself and Constance. "I said I could help him prioritize the work, look for loans and contractors. Maybe even get my hands dirty. It would be a good workout." Another pause, then he finished with, "I don't know. We'll see where it goes. He just seemed like he needed help and if he gives me the listing when it's done, it would be my first in this upper bracket price range."

Constance pulled his foot to her face and kissed his toes. "My burly contractor," she said. She flipped herself forward until she was laying on top of him. She kissed him on the lips. "Or real estate mogul. What's his name?"

"Sean," he replied.

The phone next to the bed vibrated once, then a second and a third time. It was Constance's phone. Greg never brought his to bed unless he was waiting for a call from her. She picked it up.

"Damn."

"What's wrong?" he asked. "Who is it?"

"It's Vivian. She wants me to meet her in Miami tomorrow night. It means I have to cancel parties next week." She looked up from her phone. "I have an idea. You should come with me. While I'm with her, you could get some sun on the beach. Restore that sexy tan line from last summer."

"Tsk, tsk, tsk," he chided playfully. "You know how I hate it when you tell me I *should* do something." He pushed a stray hair back from her face. "I don't really want to spend time on the beach alone. And if you're going to be busy and not need me at parties next week, I'd rather go back home."

"To see Sean," she said, pondering what that meant.

"To do something productive," he said. "Fixing up that house can only improve our own property values."

"Your real estate work is honing your sales skills, isn't? Well he's lucky to have your help." She untied his robe. "I know how you can be productive in the meantime," and she pulled off her own robe.

Chapter 10:

Sean sat on the leather sofa with the computer on his lap. The room was dark, but he had flipped on the chandelier then dimmed it to provide appropriate lighting. He heard ringing. Quickly he peeled off his t-shirt.

"Hi Sean," he heard. Maya's image appeared on the screen. She was holding her phone in front of her face.

"Hi sexy, have time for a little chat, and maybe more—wink, wink—with your loving hubby?"

"I'm at the studio. . .working, Sean."

"So late? It's after ten there."

"I'm in a zone with my work. It's going really well. And if I spend too much time at the condo, it's that much time I have to spend cleaning it for prospective buyers."

Sean didn't want to get into it about the condo. It was a sore subject. He diverted. "So work is going well? Can I see something?"

"Oh, I don't want to show you over video chat. But, yeah, I'm really happy with my direction."

She's doing great work, Sean heard through the speaker.

"That's Todd," she said.

Really great, he heard follow.

"And that's Ali?" he asked.

"You know it."

Ali face filled the screen. "Hi, Sean," she said, and waved.

"Come on," he begged. "Give me a peek."

"Hold on." She turned the camera to the canvas behind her. It was just an outline of a human. Too rough to tell if it was male or female.

"I like it," he said. "Can I see anything more finished?"

"That was your peek," she scolded. "Hey, stand up," she ordered.

He did as she said.

"Hold the computer further away so I can see your whole torso."

He obeyed, then heard a click.

"Got it," she said. "Screen shot. You may make it into my gallery of men. With the tattoos, I can show off your artwork in my art."

"Clever." He paused for a second. "Listen," he said quietly, "are you sure you don't have a storeroom, or someplace private, you can go to, so we fool around for a bit?"

We promise we won't watch, he heard Ali say.

Speak for yourself. I'd pay to see these two go at it, came from Todd.

"Nobody's going at it," said Maya to her studio mates. "Sean, I've got to get back to work, but there is one thing I want to talk to you about." She moved over to the corner away from the other two. "It's about the condo. I don't think we should sell it."

"But I won't have the money I need to flip the house unless we do."

"What if we just rented it out? We could get two or three times our monthly mortgage for it, and it will continue to appreciate. Daddy suggested it."

He hated when her father interfered with their lives, but it was an option he hadn't considered. "I need to look into what that would look like. Have you found a place for yourself yet?"

"I'm spending most nights at Todd and Ali's. It's a lot closer and they don't seem to mind having a third roommate."

"OK," he agreed. "Let me think about it. I'll talk to the agent and banker to see how it would work."

"Thanks, Sean. I'll talk to you tomorrow, OK?"

"I love you," he said before disconnecting.

"Love you too."

Love you too, came from Todd and Ali in unison.

Sean began a search for online porn.

Chapter 11:

Greg jogged up the steps in front of Sean's house. Since he'd landed, Greg had stopped by his own house, then run to the store for foods he'd been craving. Now, it was nearly four, and he was anxious to see if Sean had made any progress on the project plan.

The front door was open. Through the screen, Greg could hear voices talking and laughing. He knocked on the frame and waited. After a few seconds, he knocked again. Finally, Sean's head peeked out from the library.

"Greg," he said loudly. "What're you doing? Come on in. You're back early."

"I heard voices. I didn't just want to barge in."

Sean threw his arms around Greg. "Don't be silly, you're always welcome."

Through the library archway, Greg saw a woman sitting on the edge of a chair. It looked like the woman he'd seen outside days before.

"Greg, this is my neighbor, Katie Jo."

Greg approached her as she stood. "Hi, I'm Greg."

"Katie Jo," she said confidently, her small hand sliding into Greg's.

"Katie Jo has lived next door all her life," said Sean. "She's able to answer a shitload of questions about the family. Filling in the blanks."

"Not all my life," corrected Katie Jo. "I was married but moved back to take care of my mother after my father died."

It was more information than Greg had wanted, but he nodded in acknowledgement.

Before quiet could overtake them, Sean pointed to the scrapbooks on the table and the oversized portrait on the wall and continued, "Wait until I tell you some of the stories. I've got one fucked up family."

"I'd like to hear them," said Greg

"You know," said Katie Jo, "I should probably get going to check on Mother. You guys no doubt have catching up to do."

"Hey, I don't want to interrupt," said Greg. "I was just anxious to hear how the plan is coming, but we can do that tomorrow if you two want to keep going."

Katie Jo put her manicured hand on Greg's arm. "No, I'm sure Mother needs tending to. We can pick this up tomorrow."

She moved to hug Sean. Greg noticed she was at least a foot shorter than Sean and about as about as wide as she was tall.

After she had gone, Greg said to Sean, "Sorry I didn't call first. My phone has been acting up."

"Hey, no worries. It's great to see you, and I could sure use your help with the plan. But why are you back early?"

"Constance had a work thing she had to go to in Miami, and I told her I'd rather be back here." Greg considered his next question, but since he'd noticed Katie Jo lurking around before, he asked, "So what's the deal with the neighbor?"

"Weird, huh? She dropped in a couple of days ago and brought me some cookies."

"A regular Welcome Wagon," said Greg.

"Come on, sit down," said Sean returning himself to the sofa. "Yeah, sure not something that would happen in New York. But when she told me she grew up next door, I figured she could be a resource."

Greg sat in the chair previously occupied by Katie Jo. "Did she spend a lot of time inside? Does she remember what it looked like before the fire?"

"She grew up with my dad. Can you believe that? She's a year older, but they played together when they were young, so she was here a lot. Hey, where are my manners? Can I get you a beer or something?"

"No. No thanks." Greg had nearly forgotten his main goal in stopping by. "I do want to hear about what you've been working on. Was thinking, maybe we could go back to my place. Have some beers, grill some steaks. You could fill me in."

"That sounds great. My diet of McDonald's and cheese and crackers is getting kind of old."

"Ready to go now?"

"Yeah. Let me put some shoes on and grab my notebook."

As they walked up the Parkway toward Greg's, Sean said, "So, how was my hometown?"

"Good," said Greg. "You know this is kind of an ugly weather season. It was rainy and cold."

"It rained a bunch here," offered Sean. "Found some new leaks in the roof. Anyway, you were saying. How's Constance?"

"Same. Working all the time."

"But you love her."

Greg smiled. "I do."

"And she makes a ton of money, so that's always good," joked Sean. "More than I can say about my wife."

"I've always assumed so," said Greg, curiously. "We live very well, but I don't really ever see the financials. I guess I don't need to when I live here."

They had reached the front of his house.

"I've been wondering which one was yours," said Sean. "Nice!"

"Let's go in around back," said Greg.

They followed the steppingstone path to the back patio.

"You have a pool," remarked Sean.

"And a hot tub," said Greg. "Pool is pretty small. No good for laps but I can float on an air mattress in the summer."

"And it looks great. I love the glow of a blue pool on a warm evening."

Greg opened the French door leading to the sunroom and began the tour. The over decorated living room and dining room were in the front of the house with the view of the lake. There was a recently remodeled kitchen behind the dining room and well-used office next to that—clearly Constance's. In the foyer was a staircase with an ornate wrought iron railing, in character with the Italianate styling of the house, leading to the second floor.

Two bedrooms were in the back, beautifully appointed for guests.

"Constance considers this private space, so don't ever tell her I showed you, OK?"

Greg opened the double doors that opened on the massive master bedroom. It spanned the entire front of the house. There was a giant, king-size bed. By the windows, two sumptuous sofas. On the side, a fireplace.

"So, this is where the magic happens," joked Sean, too stunned to say anything else. "But no TV. Don't you guys ever watch porn?"

"Not together," joked Greg back. "But we do watch movies." He flipped a switch by the bed, a motor hummed, and a hatch opened in the ceiling. Next a large, flat screen descended over the foot of the bed and locked into place.

"No shit," said Sean in disbelief.

"Come on," urged Greg, climbing onto the bed. Sean hesitated only a moment before climbing on too. "We watch TV and can still see the lake."

"This is awesome," proclaimed Sean. "I want this. . .I'm sure I can't afford it, but I want it."

Greg laughed. "Like I said, we live very well. How about a beer and I fire up the grill."

In the kitchen, Greg handed Sean a cold beer and then prepped the steaks and sides. Picking up the plate of steaks, Greg said, "Let's go."

"Can I take anything?

"Yeah, if you could grab my beer and get the door."

"You got it."

Greg opened the grill and turned on the gas.

While the grill was warming up, he loaded kindling and logs into the stone fire pit. Sean settled into one of the padded chairs opposite. "Wood? Not gas?" asked Sean.

"Yeah," answered Greg. "All the fireplaces inside are wood too" He pointed to the large wood pile next to the garage. Constance insisted. She likes the crackle and the smell. And she's really good at lighting them." He laughed and added, "I think she's kind of a pyromaniac." Then he pointed to the grill, "But she let me have my way with the gas grill."

Greg struck a match and the teepee of logs ignited.

He took a swig of his beer, then Greg asked, "So, what are you thinking regarding the remodel?"

Sean opened the notebook and began reviewing his thoughts as Greg cooked the steaks.

They ate by the fire, with Greg asking questions and Sean answering as best he could. Then he had a question for Greg.

"I have a question," announced Sean.

"Blue," said Greg.

"Huh?"

"Not blue? Ok, then Two."

"What are you talking about?"

"Left."

Sean just looked at Greg, wondering if he was having a stroke.

"You said you had a question," said Greg. Those are my standard answers to all questions."

"Asshole," replied Sean.

"No sense of humor. You need another beer."

"Wait," said Sean. "I have a serious question."

Lifting his beer, Greg said, "I'm jet lagged and too fucked up for serious questions."

"Greg, listen. I need an opinion, and you're Mr. Real Estate. Maya doesn't want to sell our condo. She's suggesting that we rent it out and that I use the proceeds of that to finance the work here. That way we'll have some place to live when this is done."

"Shit," said Greg. "I kind of forgot that this project, that hasn't even started, is a short-term thing. . .and then you're back to New York."

"That's the plan," acknowledged Sean.

Greg pondered that a bit longer, then replied to the original question. "Well, that's an option. We'd need to put together a spreadsheet with your mortgage, projected rental price, association fees, utilities, wear and tear, and insurance to make sure it cash flows positive. With the equity you can refinance. The cash from that pays for at least some of this work and your rental income pays your first and second mortgage. It's all in the numbers. I can help you take a look at that."

"Damn," said Sean. "That would be great."

"Let's clean this up, then I want to show you something else."

"That's what she said," joked Sean.

"Pa dump," retorted Greg to the off-color suggestion.

A door in the kitchen led down some wooden stairs to a mostly unfinished basement.

"This looks a lot like mine," said Sean. "Any dead bodies?"

"Maybe some dead mice," said Greg. They crossed the painted concrete floor where he opened a door and flipped a light switch. "This is my man cave."

"Holy shit," said Sean, amazed. "You showed me your freaking froo froo bedroom but were holding out on this?"

"Yeah, well, it's kind of my secret."

"What a great place for you two to watch movies," remarked Sean, looking around the room.

"It's pretty much just me. Constance hates this room but allows me my indulgence since most of the rest of the house is for her work."

"You're going to have to explain her job to me some time," said Sean. "But not now. I'm too distracted by all this. And If you ever want company down here, I'm your man."

"I'll remember that," said Greg, reaching into a wooden box on one of the shelves. He pulled out a perfectly rolled joint and held it up for Sean. "This is what I wanted to come down here for. In the mood to light it up?"

"Fuck yeah," cheered Sean. "It's been forever."

"Cool, me too. Let's head back outside."

Sean took another look around the room. "I'm not sure I ever want to leave here. I'd say I want this in my house too, but I'm pretty sure this represents my entire budget."

Outside, Greg fired up the pot stick, took a long hit and handed it to Sean.

"So, tell me about Maya," said Greg. "How did you two meet, etcetera, etcetera. Oh, and about your tattoos." He did an exaggerated rolling motion with his hand to indicate he wanted the whole story. Then he reclined to take it all in.

Sean took another hit as he organized his thoughts.

"Well, you know I'm adopted," began Sean. I was in college when my parents were killed and I wanted to do something to memorialize them, so I got this small tattoo on my forearm." He pointed to a heart with the numeral three in the middle. "It was just something to say the three of us were a family."

Greg pointed to the larger tattoo snaking up Sean's arm. "I guess it grew."

"Yeah well, Thanks to Maya. I met her while I was tending bar after college. It was a gay bar downtown. She and her girlfriends came in one night. All of us bartenders were shirtless—it helps with the tips. I'd been hitting the gym hard to make the boys drool. Again, for tips." He took the joint from Greg's fingers and inhaled, before handing it back. "And she started giving me shit about my big arms and pathetic little tattoo. I challenged her to design something more elaborate. She took a Sharpie from her purse and, in between me pouring shots and beers, she started drawing. She's an artist, you know."

"So, you've said. I have yet to see her work. But this isn't Sharpie," Greg said, still tracing it with his finger."

Sean laughed. The beer and the weed were affecting him. "No, it's not. She drew for a while. It was hideous—she was drunk. But after my shift I took her back to her place and banged her to prove you don't have to be gay to work in a gay bar. We hit it off and she ended up drawing this elaborate design and came with me while I got it inked. We've been together ever since."

"Nice," said Greg. "Good story."

Greg turned to the other side to show that ink. "This is more of a fantasy image we concocted together. No real meaning. There's this ship and some sea creatures."

Greg leaned in to examine it more closely. "What's this? A squid? I like it."

"Yeah," confirmed Sean. "You have any ink that you're hiding?" asked Sean.

"No. I'd like to," admitted Greg. "But I don't know what I'd get—although I like the squid a lot. Constance doesn't really want me to though. But yours are sure sexy, so maybe she'd reconsider." He took another drag before handing the cigarette back to Sean, saying "Finish it off. I have to pee."

When Greg got back from the bathroom, Sean's head was resting on the back on the back of his chair and he was staring at the stars. "You OK?" asked Greg.

"My heads pretty fucked up," said Sean. Then he suddenly stood up. "I think the pot is making me kind of paranoid," said Sean. "I need to go."

"Maybe you should settle down first," suggested Greg. "It's probably not good to be home alone when you're feeling like this."

"I just need to go sleep," insisted Sean. "I'll be fine. Just too much of a good thing."

"Want me to walk with you?" offered Greg.

"No, I'll be fine," said Sean. "Thanks for everything, man. I'm sorry."

"I had fun. I'll stop by in the morning, OK?"

"Yeah, sounds great. I'll say *hi* to the family for you.

Chapter 12:

Greg could hear his phone's vibrating buzz across the room. He had no idea what time it was, but it was light outside and he felt like shit. He sprang from the bed with more energy than he could have expected, picking up the phone on what he counted as the fifth buzz. On the screen was a message requesting a FaceTime with Constance. He accepted and the screen filled with an image a bright blue sky and rolling waves. After a few seconds the image switched, and it was Constance's face.

"Good morning," she greeted. "Why aren't you here with me? We could be making love to the sound of the ocean."

"Good morning, Connie," he said groggily. He noticed runners outside his window and realized he was naked. He wondered if they could see him, then stepped back from the glass.

"Were you still sleeping?" she asked. "It's after nine there."

"Yeah," he said. "I guess I overslept." Changing the subject, "How's Miami?"

"My meetings are a bore, but the weather is wonderful. I so wish you were here."

Greg rubbed his eyes then pushed his hair back, scratching his scalp, before yawning.

"I guess I'm boring you," said Constance snidely.

"No, not at all," he argued. "Just trying to get my bearings." He looked at the clock to confirm her time estimate. Nine-O-Eight read the large digits.

"Did you stay up late?"

"Later than I realized, I guess. "I had Sean over for steaks on the grill. We lit the fire pit and drank some beer. He left around nine-thirty; I think. Then I watched a movie."

"Lots of guessing this morning," she said. "Do you want to go back to sleep?"

"No, no," he said. "Talk to me. What are you doing today?"

She went on about her day concluding with a scheduled dinner for the evening before asking what he'd be doing.

"I told Sean I'd come by and review his project plan with him," Greg said. "That's about it, I guess. I mean that's about it, no guessing."

"I'm done here after dinner tonight, and then I'm flying back to New York."

"Uh huh," he muttered.

"But I don't have anything scheduled there tomorrow, so I'm going to fly through Minneapolis. We can spend all day and night together before I fly on to New York."

"Great," he said, trying to sound more enthusiastic than he felt. It would be great to see her, and he was getting horny, but he was just so damn tired. "I'll pick you up. When do you get in?"

"I'm not sure yet. I'll have my assistant send you the details when she's made the arrangements."

"Great," he repeated. "Oh, have her send it to email. This phone is acting up still."

"We'll have to get that replaced," she said. After a pause, "If you just woke up, are you naked?" Let me see."

He held the phone at arm's length, including his bare chest in the image area.

96

"Lower," she ordered.

He hesitated then panned down. Even limp, his dick was impressive. He brought the phone back to his face.

"I can't wait to see you," she said. "All of you."

"Same here."

"I've got to run to brunch. I'll have a mimosa for you."

"Ahh," he said, though the idea of any alcohol at that moment made him want to vomit. "Have fun. I love you, C."

"Til tomorrow."

He disconnected and collapsed backward on the bed, mumbling, "Fuck me."

: : :

To say Sean slept poorly was being overly generous. In truth, he hadn't slept at all. He was troubled by his time with Greg. More accurately, he was troubled by the feelings he had during his time with Greg. He feigned paranoia, brought on by the weed, but the feelings were more like lust.

Sean always viewed himself as one hundred percent straight. He was confident claiming that, even when friends teased him for working in a gay bar. He hadn't had a lot of sexual experiences before hooking up with and then marrying Maya, but they were all with women. From the first time he masturbated, it was looking at Playboy. He hadn't even had any of those drunken college nights he had heard about, where roommates made out. He never consciously sneaked a peek in the locker room.

But last night, in the dark, with the firelight illuminating their faces, Sean felt inexplicably drawn to Greg. It wasn't that he was imagining what Greg looked like naked. That never crossed his mind. He just felt really close to this guy he'd only recently met. When they hugged hello or goodbye, there was a warmth that was comforting like he'd never known. That's why he'd had to get out of there. He wasn't paranoid. Well, maybe he was. . .about what he might do. He hadn't consciously thought about kissing Greg, but that seemed like the logical next step. Then what?

So, he came home. And on top of the beer and the weed, he had pulled out the scotch. He sat on the couch in the library and drank scotch. And stared at the family portrait. After an hour, maybe longer he started seeing things in it that he hadn't before. There was a dog at his father's feet. It was black with white patches. It's coloring made it disappear into to shadows.

Sean walked up to the painting to get a closer look.

"Hi, little guy," he said placing his fingers on the pup. "I'll have to look through the photos albums for more pictures of you. And I bet Katie Jo knows your name."

His fingers unconsciously started to move across a larger area of the family's visage. His fingers stopped. He felt something other than the texture of the oil paint. His middle finger poked through the canvas. There was a hole. Right there in his father's dark blue sweater. Right about where the heart would be. A hole. He held up the flashlight on his phone to examine it more closely. Then he looked across the broader canvas. He spotted no other holes.

"What the fuck? What is wrong with me?"

Sean turned off the light, tossed his phone on the table, sat back down on the worn leather couch and poured himself another scotch.

When daylight finally came, he picked up the phone and pressed dial.

"Hi, Sean," came the response from the receiver.

"Todd?" said Sean.

"Yeah, sorry. I saw it was you calling so I picked up. Maya just ran to the back but won't be a minute. Here she comes now." Muffled, "It's Sean."

"Hi, Sean."

He was relieved to hear her voice.

"What's going on?" he asked, trying not to sound desperate.

"Just working away," she answered. "Is everything OK? You sound weird."

"Yeah, uh, everything is great." He took a breath. "Uh, I talked to a friend about your idea to rent the condo. He agreed that makes some sense, so I'm going to look into it."

"Great," she said.

"Maya, can you come visit sometime soon?" he asked, just short of a beg.

"Sean, I don't see that happening. I've got so much to do before the show. I just can't take the time right now." She paused but got no reaction from him. "But you're still coming to the show, aren't you? It's just next month and we can spend some quality time together then."

"Yeah, I'm coming," he said. "I guess I should book my flight. Send me the details, OK?"

"I will. And listen, I've got to go. but call me tonight or tomorrow night. We can have some phone fun."

"OK."

99

"I'm so happy about the condo news. I just know you're going to grow tired of that remodel project and be ready to come home. I really want to have our home to come back to."

"I'm not going to *grow tired* of it," he said, mimicking her exact words."

"We'll see," she said dismissively. "Gotta run. Bye."

She disconnected before he could say anything. He didn't have anything to more say anyway.

Chapter 13:

It had taken Greg another solid hour to rally. He'd pounded an energy drink, eaten some carbs and was now on his run— slower than usual but maintaining his discipline. The first time he passed Sean's house, it looked closed up tight. By the second time around the lake, he saw that Sean's front door was open.

Greg ran the rest of the way home for a hot shower. The hot water felt good. He dressed in jeans and long-sleeved tee, adding a puffer vest and Converse sneakers. Greg stopped in the kitchen for another shot of carbonated caffeine and a granola bar. He looked out the window to the patio, noticing remnants of the previous night's barbecue. As he was dealing with the mess, he noticed Sean's marble-covered composition notebook. He sat down in the chair to look at Sean's notes. Inside Greg found a well thought out list of work to be completed. There was a priority list and even some sketches of the house's facade, a revised floorplan and details of moldings and millwork. On the edges of nearly every page, Sean had written words like *FUCK*, *I can't do this*, *I have no idea what I'm doing here*, and *HELP*.

"Hey, you forgot this," said Greg as he walked through Sean's doorway.

"Oh, wow, thanks," said Sean. "Good morning, by the way."

"Afternoon," corrected Greg.

"Damn, I guess you're right." Sean paused for a moment, then added, "Sorry I ran out last night. I. . ."

Before Sean could continue, Greg interrupted, saying, "Don't worry about it. That was some pretty strong shit. If you're not used to it, it can fuck you up pretty good."

Sean nodded.

"Glad to see you made it out the other end."

"It was a rough night," said Sean. "But all's good now. I even talked to Maya this morning."

Greg chuckled. "And I spoke with my wife. She's going to be here tomorrow. Maybe you can meet her."

"Sure. I'd like that.

Greg handed Sean the notebook. "I hope you don't mind. I took a look inside."

Sean began to blush. "And?"

"Well except for the expressions of self-doubt, I thought it was great."

"Thanks," said Sean sheepishly.

"Sean, you home?"

"Who's that?" asked Greg.

"Katie Jo," answered Sean. "Apparently she's found her way in through the back door now."

"In here," called out Sean.

Katie Jo entered the front hall. "I brought more cookies." Noticing Greg, she said, "Oh, hi Greg. I didn't know you'd be here."

"I had something to drop off too," Greg replied. Turning to Sean, he said, "I'll let you go."

"Wait," said Sean. "I was hoping to talk about this with you. Get your ideas."

"Yes, you stay," said Katie Jo. "You boys have work to do. I'm just dropping these off. I have to get back to Mother." She set the plate of cookies down on the table.

102

After Katie Jo made her exit, Greg said, "Man, she does not like me."

"Sure, she does," protested Sean. "What's not to like."

"Trust me. She does not trust me."

"Haha," said Sean. "Nice play on words, but I think you're wrong. I'll get her back here to tell some more family tales. We'll have some drinks. You'll like her."

"OK," agreed Greg. "Let's talk about your ideas."

: : :

It was always a difficult choice. Airport pickup at the curb or park and meet inside. Inside was more romantic, but curbside more efficient. Greg opted for efficient but brought a small bouquet of red tulips to up the romance a bit.

Greg parked the Jag at the curb and got out. Immediately, the airport rent-a-cop reprimanded him.

"I'm picking up my wife," protested Greg. "She's right here."

Constance was moving toward him in a black and red flower print dress and matching raincoat. Black patent leather heels completed the outfit.

He moved toward her to help with the Louis Vuitton roller bag and was reprimanded again. When the mock cop looked toward her, she winked at him and everything was fine. After the bag was loaded in the back seat, Greg opened her door. But, before she could enter, he turned her around and kissed her. One more stern look from the uniformed young man and they were off.

"You look wonderful," Greg said.

"Thanks," she answered. "And thank you for the flowers. Red, they match my outfit.

"New?" he asked.

"Without you to distract me I had some free time to shop. I did quite a bit of damage at the South Beach boutiques."

"Anything for me?"

"You'll see," she said playfully.

As they were approaching home, they came upon Sean's house.

"This is it," Greg said pointing toward the gray box on the hill. Noticing Sean, he said, "Sean's here. Let's stop."

"Oh, Greg," she argued. "Not now. I just got off a four-hour flight."

"I already told you, you look wonderful. Just a quick hello. Aren't you curious to see the place?"

He stopped at the curb. She didn't move.

"He's already seen us," said Greg. "It would be rude not to go up."

She looked annoyed as she reached for the door handle. Greg rushed around to help her, but she was already out and headed toward the crumbling concrete steps.

From the top, Sean called out, "Be careful on the steps. I'm insured, but still."

Greg took Constance's hand, then called back to Sean, "So you talked to the insurance guy?"

"Yeah. Fixing these suckers got moved way up on the priority list."

"Hi Constance, I'm Sean," he said when she reached the top. He reached out his hand in greeting.

"Nice to meet you," she replied.

"And I'm Greg," he said, with a chuckle.

"Welcome to Chez Miller slash Donaldson." Sean's hand extended to the house.

"Oh, it's Miller slash Donaldson now," joked Greg.

"The Donaldsons raised me and loved me, and they get at least equal billing. Except for some random Miller sperm and a random egg, I'm all Donaldson. The Miller's never even acknowledged I existed. If it weren't for a silly DNA test my connection to this house and family would have been lost forever."

Greg held up his hands, "Okay, I surrender. I've got no loyalty to the Miller name or legacy. Miller slash Donaldson it is."

"I hear you've taken on quite a large project," said Constance to change the subject.

"What has he told you?" asked Sean jokingly.

"He's told me quite a lot. . .about the house. . .about you."

"We only have a few minutes," said Greg. Give us a quick tour?"

"Sure, sure."

Inside, the foyer was impressive, but old. Sean led them into the living room. Constance laughed when she saw it.

"Oh, I'm sorry," she said about her reaction. "You boys are too young to remember when this was tres chic. I don't know what we were thinking."

"Hey, I'm not that young," said Greg. "I may not have been around when it was new, but there was still a lot of shag carpeting at my friends' houses growing up."

Sean said, "The dining room and kitchen are similar. It's what they did after the fire."

"Oh, a fire. How awful," said Constance.

"It killed Sean's grandmother," added Greg before immediately regretting it.

"I'm so sorry," offered Constance.

"It's not like I knew her," Sean replied flippantly. "Anyway, across the way is the library. It's the cool, old style."

"Classic," said Constance. "Is this how you plan to restore the house?"

"Ideally," said Sean. "At least eventually. It all comes down to budget and saving the place from the wrecking ball."

"Too many of these old houses have been torn down," said Constance. "I've watched it and hate nearly everything put up to replace them. I hope you're successful."

"We should go," said Greg. "Constance had a late night and long flight."

"I understand," said Sean. "I'm glad you stopped though. It was so nice to meet you Constance. This guy has done nothing but sing your praises but somehow still fell short."

"Aren't you the charmer," replied Constance. "I'd say he didn't do you justice as well."

Sean went in for a hug. She accepted only a partial. Then he threw his arms around Greg, whispering in his hear, "I think she likes me."

Greg laughed, slapped Sean's arms, saying, "We'll talk. I'll stop by in a couple of days after taking Connie back to the airport."

Katie Jo came in from the back. "Don't forget about the seance."

"Hi, I'm Katie Jo," she said offering her hand to Constance. "The nosy neighbor."

"Uh, hello, Katie Jo," replied Constance.

"They were just heading home," said Sean.

"Well I'm glad I got to say *hi*, at least."

"Same here," said Constance, learning of Katie Jo for the first time. "Seance?"

"She's joking," said Sean. "KJ has lived next door most of her life. She knew my family so she's providing me some family lore."

"We're planning to get together one evening," said Greg. "To hear some stories over a bottle of wine."

"Ghost stories," joked Katie Jo.

"Sounds like fun," said Constance, insincerely. And then more snidely, "Like Scout camp."

"Let's go," said Greg.

Back in the car, Greg asked, "Well? Did you like him?"

"What's not to like," said Constance. "He's a taller, better looking version of you."

"Ouch," said Greg.

"How's he hung?"

"I have no idea," replied Greg.

"Good. What about that woman, though?"

"Yeah, she's kind of odd," admitted Greg. "Super nice, but something seems off."

"I mean her shape," said Constance. "Honestly one the strangest body types. Her hands and feet are so dainty, but the rest of her."

"I never noticed her hands or feet."

"And I'm sorry, but the white capri pants and fitted sweater? They were expensive but totally wrong for her."

Anxious to move on, Greg said, "But you liked Sean?"

"Of course," she replied, wondering why her approval was so important to him. "He has an awfully large project ahead of

107

him. You know I'm not giving you up completely and indefinitely."

"I know," he said, pulling into the garage. "Now let's go inside so I can ravage you."

"About time!"

Chapter 14:

"You made it," said Sean as Greg sprinted up the front steps.

"Of course," said Greg. "What're you doing sitting out here?"

"Katie Jo is setting up in there," answered Sean. "She makes kind of a big deal about everything."

Greg nodded and sat on the stoop next to Sean.

"So how was it?" asked Sean.

"Constance? Great! I dropped her at the airport around three then went for my lake run."

"Are you all chafed?"

"From Constance or the run?"

"Either. Both?"

Greg punched Sean's shoulder before replying. "A little, but her company makes a really good moisturizer, so it'll be all better soon. I'll get you some."

"No need. My wife's AWOL. I ain't gettin any."

"It's great for self-pleasuring too," said Greg.

"First-hand experience?" punned Sean.

"So to speak," replied Greg.

"Sold! Economy size, please."

Greg laughed.

"Come on in, gentlemen," invited Katie Jo, as she ushered them into the library.

"That's a lot of candles," said Greg. "There must be over a hundred."

"I love the glow of a flame," she said. "But it had to be bright enough to see the photo albums."

"Just be careful," joked Sean. "We know the place is highly flammable."

"Champagne?" offered Katie Jo.

"Yes," Greg and Sean said in unison, retrieving stemmed flutes from the table.

For the next four hours they drank the bubbly wine as Katie Jo turned pages in the photo albums that Sean pulled from the shelves. Some years were well documented others had little to show. There were pictures of the family's department store as it grew from a single unit to more than fifteen. Many more pictures of the men. Great grandpa Chester as a young man. Grandpa Carl. Sean's dad Collin. Sean was most interested in the progression of his father through the years.

"Why aren't there more pictures of the women of the family? Were they camera shy?" asked Greg. "I mean, would you know?"

"Oh, I know," said Katie Jo at Greg's inference. "Women often hate how they look in pictures and avoid the camera—at least before the age of endless selfies and instant editing. But in this case, they all died pretty young."

"What do you mean?" asked Sean.

"Well you must have seen the obituaries in the scrap books," answered Katie Jo.

"No, but I'll look," said Sean.

"Well, Chester's wife—I think her name was Grace—she had another child after Carl, but she and the little girl died in childbirth. You know Carl's first wife died in the house fire when Collin was quite young. And Carl was only married to Mitzi for a couple of years when she died of a heart attack. Your dad, Collin, never wanted to get married because of it."

"Really?" said Sean. "That's sad."

"Oh, he had plenty of fun," explained Katie Jo. "Lots of girlfriends. He was a randy one. But whenever any of them suggested marriage, it was over."

"Did he have a type," asked Greg.

"There were a lot of cute blondes," replied Katie Jo. "But that's all we've got here. We're all Swedes and Norwegians." She sipped her wine, and thought for a moment, before adding, "But I do remember one dark haired girl in his grade who he liked a lot. She might have been the one that broke his heart."

"What do you mean?" asked Sean.

"Your dad was pretty irresistible," said Katie Jo. "I admit I may have had a little crush on him, even though he was a year younger—you do remind me a lot of him. Rich, handsome, smart. . .he was in demand. There were a lot of broken hearts."

"And apparently one unwanted pregnancy," said Sean, solemnly.

Greg shook Sean's shoulder, saying, "Well I'm glad he got some girl pregnant."

"Did you know her?" asked Sean.

"No," said Katie Jo. "You're thirty, so I would still have been married and living in Maine at the time. I think that was when Collin was living in New York. We weren't really in touch. He came home about the same time I did and that's when we reconnected."

"Why was he in New York?" asked Sean.

"Like everyone," said Katie Jo. "He went to make a name for himself, separate from the family. He was looking for

111

something to invest in. Probably just wanted to get away for a while."

"And do you know why he came back?" asked Greg.

"Rehab," answered Katie Jo, bluntly. "He was pretty messed up on drugs." More solemnly, she added, "Your granddad tracked him down and brought him back to clean up. But dear Collin couldn't stop himself."

"I think I've heard enough for tonight," announced Sean. He was staring at a picture of his dad when he would have been about Sean's age. Not long before he OD'd.

"I should get back to mother anyway," said Katie Jo. "I hope I didn't upset you."

"No, it's OK," said Sean. "I'm OK. I just want to take some time to go through the scrap books now that I have some more background." He finally looked up at her, saying, "Thanks, KJ."

"You're welcome, sweetie." She stood up. "Be careful with the candles. I'll collect them tomorrow."

"Thanks again," said Sean.

Greg stood up.

"Hey man, can you hang around for a while?" asked Sean.

"Sure, what's up?"

"I'm just kind of freaked out right now. Too much information. I'm having trouble processing. And I'm kind of spooked by the house right now too."

"OK," said Greg.

"Want a scotch?" asked Sean.

"I'll get it," said Greg. He grabbed the bottle and two glasses.

"Don't forget glasses for my men," said Sean, pointing to the guys in the portrait.

"You must have a hell of a liquor bill," joked Greg to lighten the mood. "I hope these guys appreciate it."

The moonlight cascaded through the window. Sean laid down at one end of the sofa, Greg sat at the other.

Swirling the caramel colored liquid in the glass, Sean said, "You know, I read the obituaries."

"What do you mean?" asked Greg.

"I told Katie Jo I hadn't seen them, but I had. I was curious whether she had any further detail. They all died in the house."

"Seriously?" questioned Greg. "But Chester's wife died in childbirth."

"It was a long time ago. Apparently, she went into labor during a snowstorm. She couldn't get to the hospital. The doctor couldn't get here. There were complications and both died."

"Wow," said Greg. "That's sad."

"That's not it though."

"What do you mean?" asked Greg.

"The men all died here too. . .although Chester and Carl at least grew to be old men first."

"That is freaky, isn't it," concurred Greg. "How did Chester die?"

"Chester, in his sleep," said Sean. "Old age. He was ninety-two."

"So, he was living here with Carl and his family."

"He built the house. Raised his son here. I don't suppose he wanted to leave it."

"And Collin OD'd here?" asked Greg.

113

"The obituary says he died at home. There's no mention of drugs or an overdose, but that's what I suspected, and Katie Jo just confirmed it."

"I'm sorry," said Greg. "But at least old Carl left you this kick-ass place."

"Kick-ass, haunted place," corrected Sean.

"Haunted?" asked Greg. "What makes you say that?"

Just then all the candles flickered.

"See?" said Sean. "Everyone who ever lived in this house, died in this house. How can it not be haunted?"

Greg let that sink in for a moment. That was a troubling truth. But the mood needed to be lightened. "I think that just means we need to blow these out." A minute later, slightly out of breath from having blown out one hundred candles, Greg said, "Again, I'm sorry about the tragic family history."

"No need," said Sean, swigging the rest of his scotch before standing up. "Again, it's not like I knew any of these people."

"That's their loss," said Greg.

"Thanks, bud," said Sean opening his arms to hug Greg. "I think I want to call Maya now. OK?"

"I'll check in with you in the morning," said Greg. "Have a good night."

"You too," said Sean. "And next time we're doing a deep dive on your family secrets."

"It was just mom and me, but I'll see what I can dig up," joked Greg as he walked out the door.

Chapter 15:

When Greg woke up, he felt like getting his hands dirty. He found a pair of old jeans in the closet. They had a few holes and were a little tighter than the last time he wore them, but they fit the role. He slipped on a white crew-neck t-shirt and fleece pullover, and the new Redwing workbooks he'd ordered. He looked in the mirror and declared himself read to work. But first, breakfast and a quick text to Sean.

When he picked up his phone in the kitchen, it was dead. He headed upstairs to retrieve the charger as the doorbell rang. It was a private messenger with a small package addressed to him.

"You live here?" asked the messenger, assessing Greg's attire.

"I do," declared Greg.

"Nice house."

"Thanks. Is that for me?"

"Greg Piersol?"

"Yep."

"Sign here."

Greg signed and the messenger turned to head back to his van. A few steps down the walk he looked back. Greg waved and winked. The guy stumbled, as he waved back, just as Greg was closing the door.

"What's this?" Greg said to himself as he headed back to the kitchen.

He grabbed a small knife from the block to cut the tape. Inside was an iPhone box. The cellophane was missing so Greg lifted the cover. Inside was the newest model, with a note.

I hate not being able to reach you. To make it easy I had one of the tech guys set it up for you. It's ready to go. Call me when you get this. Love, C.

Greg told Siri to call Connie and it began to ring. As it rang, he glanced at his old phone. It wasn't dead, it no longer had cell service. That had been transferred to the new device.

"Did you get it?"

"Good thing," said Greg. "My old phone stopped working this morning."

"I wanted to surprise you," she replied. "Do you like it?"

"I like that it works. . .and will probably hold a charge. I haven't had a chance to check out what's new and different yet. But, thank you! You saved me a trip to the Apple store."

"I know how you hate dealing with the 'geniuses'."

"That I do."

"Oh, look at the time," she said. "I have to run. Let's FaceTime tonight."

"Thanks again," he said. "I love it. I love you."

"Love you too. Bye."

Greg grabbed a juice and a bagel and headed to Sean's. When he got there, he found Sean at the desk in the library.

"Hey, stud," said Sean. "I like the outfit. Are you my new laborer?"

"Ready to work."

"My gym shorts and sweatshirt aren't going to cut it are they?"

"Well," said Greg. "I'd at least recommend boots over flip-flops."

"Noted," said Sean. "I've been looking up general contractors. I set up appointments with a couple of them for tomorrow. Can you join me?"

116

"Sure. Have you figured out the scope of work yet?"

"Just the list you already saw. I just want to get an idea of what they can do and how they charge. One of them has design/build services. It's more educational than anything at this point."

"OK. Makes sense. What about today? Want to rip up that god-awful shag carpet?"

"That seems like a good place to start," said Sean gleefully.

"Actually, I think the place we need to start is the hardware store. We're going to need some tools."

"Let me put on pants and shoes."

"I didn't bring the Jag," said Greg. "Can you drive?"

"I turned in the rental car," answered Sean. "But Granddad's old Lincoln is in the garage, and the beast still runs."

"Let's do it."

After the hardware store, they picked up lunch. Sean had a hard time navigating the Lincoln through the narrow drive thru. They parked at the far end of the parking lot to eat their burgers, fries and Cokes. Greg showed Sean his new iPhone.

Back at the house, they got to work. Greg worked up a sweat so removed the fleece.

"Give me that new phone," said Sean.

"Why?"

"Just give it to me."

Greg removed the phone from his pocket, held it in front of his face to unlock it, then handed it to Sean.

"What are you doing? asked Sean.

"Grab the edge of the carpet and flex," said Sean.

A second later Sean had snapped several pictures of his friend hard at work.

"If you ever want to get Constance hot and bothered," said Sean. One of these should do the trick."

Greg laughed. "I'll save it for just the right moment."

They had pulled up all the carpet, cut it into manageable segments, and tied them into rolls.

The sun was starting to set when Sean said, "I'm beat. Can we call it a day?"

"Sounds good to me," agreed Greg. "We can work on removing the pad tomorrow."

"Nope," said Sean. "We're interviewing contractors."

"What time?

"One at eleven and the other at one-thirty."

"Well, maybe after the second one," suggested Greg.

"Keeping me on task," said Sean. "I like it. Hey, thanks for your help today. Sorry you tore your shirt."

Greg played with the four-inch opening across his ribs. "I've got more of these. Given our progress, I'd say it was worth it. And I had fun."

"Want a beer?" offered Sean.

"Nah," said Greg. "I skipped my run this morning. I want to try to get it in."

"You're supposed to be the old man between the two of us."

"Oh, I am," said Greg. "You just haven't hit the point where you have to work to stay fit. It will come my young friend. It will come."

"I know, and I dread it," replied Sean. "I feel like I've already spent a lifetime in the gym."

Greg peeled off his leather work gloves and fist pumped Sean. "I'll come by a little before eleven?"

"Sounds good. Have a good run and a good night."

: : :

Sean and Greg waited for the first contractor to arrive. Not surprisingly, he was late.

Greg was wearing the same jeans as yesterday and a fresh t-shirt. Sean had adopted a similar look, with a gray t-shirt instead. V-neck.

"Here," said Sean as he tossed Greg a plastic bag.

"What is it?" asked Greg.

"Look inside," commanded Sean.

Greg laughed as he pulled out a new three-pack of t-shirts.

"A little thank you, and compensation for a lost comrade," said Sean.

"You didn't need to do this," said Greg. "And I'll definitely wear that shirt again. It makes me look kind of rugged, I think. Just need to wash it first. It reeked when I took it off."

"It reeked before you took it off," joked Sean.

"Nice," said Greg. "Thanks again, man." Then Greg asked, "So have you seen Katie Jo since the other night?"

"No," answered Sean. "She's been laying kind of low. Maybe I freaked her out."

The doorbell rang and Sean answered it. Four hours later, they had interviewed two contractors and were working on removing carpet pad while they discussed the takeaways from those meetings.

"Well, that was depressing," said Sean. "No way I can afford either of those guys, much less the work that needs to be done."

"You positioned it as a learning exercise," counseled Greg. "From that perspective it was successful. Now you have some information and can consider other options."

"I'm just not sure we should be pulling up this carpet," said Sean. "Maybe I shouldn't be doing any work. Not spending any money."

"Maybe," agreed Greg. "But the carpet isn't going to affect the sale price one way or the other if you decide to sell. We might as well stay busy in the meantime."

"I guess," said Sean. "Man, it's fucking hot in here." He wiped his brow on the sleeve of his t-shirt.

"It's gotten warm outside," said Greg. "We should have picked up a fan when we were at the store yesterday. The old man must have one somewhere. Want me to look?"

"Sure," said Sean. "I'm going to try to open a window at least."

Greg was rummaging through the storage room off the kitchen when he heard the sound of breaking glass.

Sean screamed, "FUCK!"

Greg ran into the living room. Sean was holding his wrist. Blood was streaming down his arm.

"What happened?" asked Greg.

"I was trying to lift the window. I guess the sash is rotten. The handles just broke right off and my arm went through the pane."

"Let me see," said Greg.

Just then, Katie Jo, walked in the room from the back, "Sean are you in here?"

"KJ, he's hurt," said Greg frantically. Pointing to the unopened t-shirts, he said, "Quick, grab one of those so I can wrap up his wrist. We need to get him to the emergency room."

"No medical insurance," said Sean. "It will be OK. I'll just keep pressure on it."

"It's probably going to need stitches," suggested Katie Jo. "Urgent care is closer. And cheaper."

Greg got the shirt secured on Sean's arm. Turning to Katie Jo, he asked, "Can you drive?"

"I'll just run home and get my keys. Meet me in the alley."

Greg and Sean crawled in the back of Katie Jo's Cadillac.

"Nice car," said Sean. "New? Smells new. Fuck, this hurts."

"New enough that I don't want your blood all over it," she joked to keep him distracted. "Keep your DNA to yourself."

An hour later, Sean had twelve stitches in his left arm, a Band-Aid on his right hand, a plastic bag with a bloody t-shirt sealed in it, and a credit card receipt with Greg's card number on it.

"I'll pay you back, man," he said to Greg.

"Don't worry about it. I'm just glad you're going to be alright, even if it means no manual labor for a while."

"I've had enough blood, sweat and tears for the month."

"Good thing the month is almost over," joked Greg. "But May first it's back to work for you. In the meantime, as we talked about, ponder your options."

"One option I'd like to ponder is dinner," said Sean. "Pretty sure I'm not supposed to take these pain pills on an empty stomach."

"And with no alcohol," mothered Katie Jo.

"Killjoy," rebutted Sean. "But seriously, how about dinner. Me and my two saviors. My treat."

Greg looked at Katie Jo, then at Sean. "Sounds good to me. Any suggestions, KJ?"

"Is calling me KJ going to be a thing?" she asked.

"Mom, dad, don't fight," joked Sean.

"Is that a problem?" asked Greg. "It's just shorter."

"No problem," she replied. "Let's go. I've got a place in mind."

Two hours later, Katie Jo pulled the Cadillac through the alley stopping at Sean's back gate.

"Here you go, boys," she said. "Thanks for dinner. And Sean, you've got my number. . .let me know if you need anything. I'll check on you tomorrow."

"Thanks, Katie Jo," replied Sean. "It's nice having a friendly neighbor."

"G'night, KJ," said Greg.

"You know, the KJ thing is growing on me," she answered.

After Katie Jo pulled away, Sean asked Greg, "Got time to come in for a minute?"

"Sure. I wanted to help you get settled anyway."

Sean sat down heavy on the sofa. "Let's get this thing off," he said, unhooking the sling that held his left arm. "I could use a scotch."

"You're not supposed to drink," scolded Greg.

"That's only if I take the painkillers," corrected Sean.

"You don't want the drugs?" asked Greg. "The doctor didn't give you anything?"

"He numbed up my arm, but no pills. And you've been with me since they filled the prescription. I haven't taken any. It doesn't hurt." He was waving his arm around.

"OK," agreed Greg. "You're a big boy. It's up to you. But let me do one thing first. . .tape some cardboard over that broken window to help keep the cold and the bugs out."

When he came back in the room, Greg poured two glasses and added three more for the rest of the Miller men.

"I wanted to ask you something," said Sean.

"Yeah? What's that?"

"Maya has her show in a couple of weeks. Friday after next. Any chance you're going to be in New York? I'd love it if you could come. You and Constance. I want to make sure she's got enough support."

"Sure, I get it." Greg checked the calendar on his phone. "I will be in New York. I don't see anything scheduled with Constance. I'll plan on being there. When I talk to Constance, I'll check her plans and let you know."

"Thanks, bud. New phone?"

"Yeah, it came today. I showed it to you earlier. Remember?" said Greg. "A little gift from Constance. She likes to be able to reach me and my old flaky phone was making her crazy." After a pause, Greg asked, "Are you sure you didn't take any of those pain pills?"

Sean laid down. "Maybe." He smiled.

"It's late," said Greg. "No more scotch. Remember you have a history of addiction in your family. You should head up to bed."

"I sleep down here," said Sean. "Remember? Been doing it the last week or so. So, I can be close to the guys if they want to talk to me."

"They talk to you regularly?" joked Greg. "Think you might be going a little crazy?"

"Oh, I think that ship has sailed. Crazy is a given. Diagnosis confirmed. And this couch is damn comfortable."

"Well, remember to keep the arm elevated. To minimize any bleeding."

"Yes, doctor," replied Sean. He saluted with his right hand and placed the left on his chest.

"I'll come by in the morning and have an answer for you on New York." But Sean was already asleep and lightly snoring.

Part 2

Chapter 16:

Two weeks later, on Friday evening, about seven-forty, Greg and Constance walked into the Soho gallery where Maya's pieces were hanging. Both had dressed for the occasion. Greg was wearing black jeans, a dark gray button-up shirt, and a black leather jacket. Constance had on black gabardine wide-leg pants with a satin stripe down the side, a tight, long sleeve deep vee top covered in tiny silver sequins—cleavage on display, and her new red soled Louboutin, stiletto heels.

Inside the door, Greg surveyed the room for Sean. He spotted his young friend in the second room back and grabbed Constance's hand to lead her there.

"Greg," shouted Sean when he came into view. Sean spread his arms wide to embrace Greg. Greg returned the action. "Thanks for coming."

Stepping back, Greg pulled Constance forward, "Constance, you remember Sean."

Constance reached her hand to shake Sean's. Sean took it.

"Good to see you again," said Constance. "And such an exciting night for you."

"Yes," agreed Sean.

Pausing to look at both of them, Sean said, "You guys look great."

Greg felt the need to comment on Sean's appearance too. Sean was wearing tight jeans, a light blue cotton V-neck sweater that hung nicely his shoulders and pecs, and a pair of shiny, black loafers, no socks. "You're looking pretty handsome yourself." Greg rubbed Sean's shoulder. Constance took note of the familiarity between the two. After too long a pause, Greg finally said, "So where's Maya? We'd love to meet her and see her work."

Sean looked around the room and spotted Maya speaking to an older couple. "Ah. Over here," he said.

As it became apparent which one was Maya, Greg and Constance both stared at her outfit. She was wearing black, over-the-knee boots, leggings and a long black sweater that was nearly transparent. She wore no bra and the slight curve of her breasts and dark nipples were fully exposed. Only after their eyes moved up did they notice that she had a plain, but pretty face, shoulder length black hair, dark red lipstick, light mascara and large diamond studs in her ears, which Constance immediately recognized as being real. . .and expensive. Greg struggled to associate Maya's look with the Bohemian Sean had described. To him she was bordering on goth.

"Constance, Greg, this is the artist, Maya," introduced Sean. He was deliberate about not referring to her as his wife, especially in this, *professional* context.

Greg was the first to move forward. He had a hard time maintaining eye contact as he leaned in to shake Maya's hand. "Very nice to finally meet you," he said.

She curtly said, "Thank you."

Next Constance joined in, asking, "So which of all these wonderful pieces is yours?"

"These three over here," she said, gesturing with her hand to the far wall.

The four stepped closer. Greg immediately noticed the three male nudes. The male on the far left, Greg identified as

Sean. It was from behind, and the squid from the mariner tattoo was winding around further than Greg had seen before, but the shape of the shoulders and head was unmistakably Sean. "Nice ass," Greg joked. Constance took notice of the comment but said nothing.

The second painting was a reclining, dark skinned man, fully nude although the groin area was lacking the detail of the face and chest. It was almost as if she ran out of time as opposed to leaving it to the imagination. Greg was wondering who this was, when a fellow came up behind them, saying, "Isn't she awesome? My abs never looked so good. I'm Todd, by-the-way, one of Maya's studio partners."

Painting number three was unidentifiable, not just because Greg likely didn't know the man, but because he was up to his waist in water with his hands in front of this face. Nevertheless, it was a sexy look. Greg was impressed. Sean had told him she had moved on to painting human forms, but this was not what he expected. And she was good!

"These are wonderful," exuded Constance. She always had business on her mind, so it was no surprise to Greg when she asked, "Are you having success with the buyers?"

"Mine sold," said Todd, proudly, waving his champagne glass. "Some boy or girl is getting some two-dimensional Todd."

"And I have someone interested in this one," added Maya, pointing to the mystery man.

Constance turned to Greg, asking, "Would you like me to buy Sean for you?"

Greg turned bright red from embarrassment. "Out of line, Constance," he whispered.

Then noticing Todd's champagne glass, Constance said, "Oh, there's champagne. Maya, come with me to the bar. I have a business idea I'd like to discuss." Maya hesitated for a moment before the two women disappeared across the room, leaving Greg and Sean with Todd.

Looking Greg up and down, Todd said, "We need to get you added to the collection." He looked back at his image for a moment before saying, "I've got to run. See you boys around."

"Gay, right?" asked Sean after Todd had walked away.

"I wouldn't be so sure," said Greg. "Why?"

"Well he's one of Maya's studio partners. He and Ali have a place together and Maya moved in with them after the condo rented."

"So maybe he and Ali are a couple," suggested Greg.

"Definitely not," argued Sean. "No question, Ali is a loud and proud lesbian."

"So, you're worried Maya is sleeping with Todd? Maybe she's hot for Ali?"

"Not funny, asshole. It's just that I assumed I'd be staying at their place," said Sean. "But she told me there wasn't room and I should get a hotel room."

"That probably just means she wants privacy with you," said Greg.

"Maybe. I mean I assume so. We haven't gotten that far in the discussion. Either way, I'm headed back to Minneapolis tomorrow. I don't want to waste another $500 on the hotel even if she's in it with me."

"Hmm. I think you need a drink," said Greg. "Let's go to the bar."

"Agreed, just not the same one as them," said Sean.

Greg put his hand on Sean's neck and steered him through the crowd to the bar in the next room. Drinks in hand, Greg and Sean found a corner to talk.

"She's very talented," offered Greg.

Yeah, I know," agreed Sean.

"When did you pose for the painting?"

"I didn't," said Sean. "I think it's a composite of some photos she had. And memory. She has seen my bare ass a few times."

"Well, not to freak you out or anything, but I've got to say, you look really hot in it. Not that you don't always. I mean, look at you." Greg took a sip of his drink, uncomfortable with his own comments.

"Thanks man," said Sean appreciating the support, and clinking Greg's glass.

Changing the subject, Greg said, "That's some outfit Maya's got on."

"She doesn't leave much to the imagination, does she?" laughed Sean. "I told her she should skip the leggings and wear a G-string . . . or nothing at all."

"Ouch," said Greg. "It is a sexy, very Avant Garde look though."

"No shit," agreed Sean. "I've been hard all evening. If I do get her back to the hotel . . . Well, let's just leave it there."

Greg now clinked Sean's glass, "And good luck with that." They both chuckled.

"She's . . . Maya, is different than I expected," said Greg.

"How so?" asked Sean.

"I don't know. You said Bohemian, so I guess I was expecting more earthy. But the clothes, the makeup. The diamonds."

129

"The outfit and the make-up are just part of a role she's playing, I think," said Sean. "You know, eccentric artist. And the earrings, well, they're a rather sore point with us."

"How so?" asked Greg, draining his cocktail.

"She wore them for her parents. They were here earlier. They don't like me much. That's why they encouraged us to elope when they couldn't talk her out of marrying me. They didn't want to have to introduce me to their friends at a big wedding. That's why they gave us the down payment for the condo, saying it was what they would have had to spend on a reception, etc."

"I'm not making the connection to the diamonds," said Greg. "Is that instead of a big engagement ring or something?"

"No, she didn't want a diamond engagement ring. Not that I could have afforded to give her one big enough to satisfy her parents." Sean took the final sip from his glass, before adding, "The earrings were our wedding gift from them."

Greg laughed out loud. "What? Were you each supposed to wear one?"

"I asked Maya the same thing. She got pissed. She said it was their way of giving us an asset—something that would retain its value and we could sell if we ever needed money." Sean paused for a moment, then added, "They assumed we'd need money . . . until I got the big marketing job. Then I was worthy . . . until I got fired. Then I was shit again."

"So, she wears them why?" asked Greg.

"She only wears them when she sees her parents or wants to impress someone. With her parents, it's usually only when she wants something. With everyone else, it's her insecurities peeking through."

"Like tonight, what is she looking for?"

"Mostly their approval," said Sean. "And their contacts."

"Sorry I missed them. I think we might have had a nice chat. One more kind of sensitive question."

Sean looked at Greg cautiously, "Shoot."

"She wore that top in front her parents?" asked Greg.

This time Sean laughed loud enough for everyone to turn. Catching himself, he leaned into Greg to whisper.

"Never! She was wearing a jacket earlier. It strategically covered the naughty bits."

Greg just smirked.

Then Sean added, "When I asked her about the sweater earlier, she said it was no big deal because my tits were bigger than hers."

"So are mine," joked Greg. Then holding up his empty glass he said, "Should we get another drink and look for the females?"

: : :

Back in the main gallery, the guys found Maya and Constance. All three of her paintings had red stickers over the price tag indicating they were sold. Noticing this, Sean wrapped his arms around Maya, saying, "Congratulations, babe." She smiled proudly then kissed his lips. From Greg's perspective there did not appear to be any relationship issues festering. Sean was just being a little paranoid.

"So, who gets to look at my ass for all eternity?" asked Sean.

"A couple from Vancouver," responded Maya. "They're in town for the weekend and just happened to be walking by. Something about the squid caught their eye."

"So, I should stop doing squats and just keep getting inked."

Greg saw her pat Sean's ass, as she said, "Keep doing both."

"Maybe I'd look good with a squid," said Greg as he turned to Constance.

"Don't even think about it," she replied. "We should get going," said Constance to Greg. Turning to Maya, she said, "Think about what I proposed, Maya. Then let's have drinks next week."

"I will," said Maya, squeezing Sean's hand.

"Nice meeting you, again, Sean," said Constance. "Next time we'll let these two go off together so you and I can get to know each other."

"Sounds like a plan," replied Sean.

"Call me before you leave tomorrow," whispered Greg to Sean.

Sean winked as Greg and Constance walked out the door.

Chapter 17:

Constance suggested they get a light bite to eat at a neighborhood restaurant before heading home to the condo. She had a rule forbidding talking about people in public. It was too risky. She was always worried about who was listening. Instead of dishing about Maya, which was what Greg preferred in the moment, they talked about plans for the summer. Constance reviewed her schedule. It was going to be a busy one and she'd need him at her side for much of it. Then she reminded him of their plans to visit Amalfi in late July for her birthday. It was one of the many trips she'd been awarded by her company over the years. Normally he relished the first-class travel and the one-on-one time with her, but he was concerned about leaving Sean without guidance. Over dessert, he told her about the work he and Sean had planned, what they'd accomplished so far, and how good it feels to be busy . . .you know, physically. He was hoping for a compromise on his time commitment to her.

After dinner, they walked the few blocks back to the condo, and as soon as they got inside their door, Greg blurted out, "Can you believe that top?"

He laughed out loud, Constance maintained a reserve.

"I mean what's the point of wearing anything?" he continued. "Just show up naked and let your boobs hang out. Or in her case, not. Sean was mortified."

They had made their way to the bedroom as Greg was ranting. As she leaned against the wall to remove a shoe, Greg ran his finger up the contour of her cleavage. "This is the way to show off your assets," he complimented.

"I thought she looked darling. And what do you care what she wears?" Then Constance sighed, and said, "Unfortunately, some women—and men—feel that the only way to be remembered is to be outrageous. Fashion, hair, words. It's not my personality. Despite how it appears, it's likely a sign of insecurity. I guess I'm more confident, and more subtle in my duplicity. She is a sweet young woman, and I did enjoy her art."

Greg removed his shirt and tossed it on the bed. Constance picked it up and disappeared into her closet. Greg removed the rest of his clothes and slid into the bed. Through the open-door Constance continued to talk.

"I asked Maya if she'd like to display some of her pieces at one of my parties. I think my guests would enjoy her subject matter. I mean who doesn't like a naked man, even if it's a painting. Our products could be very complementary."

Greg didn't respond. He was laying on his back staring at the ceiling. His hand was on his chest and it rode up and down with each breath. He heard her talking but wasn't paying much attention. When Constance came back into the bedroom, she was wearing the shirt Greg had on all evening. He recognized it immediately as one of her signals. He wasn't in trouble, she wanted to be surrounded in his scent, but she was telling him she wasn't interested in having sex. He admitted to himself, he was relieved. He loved Constance but he was distracted.

As Constance crawled into the bed next to him, he said, "If you don't need me for anything in the next couple days, I think I'd like to head back home tomorrow."

She turned off the light, rolled onto her side and said, "You should."

Her lack of resistance concerned him.

: : :

Sean had booked a hotel in Times Square. Locals avoided the tourist traps, but he wasn't feeling like a local at the moment and he craved the activity. Maya joined him at the hotel. All the way there she had talked nonstop. She was on high from the evening and her success, and Sean was committed to help her keep it. He opened the minibar and pulled out the small bottle of champagne that cost five times what it should.

"How about a drink?" he suggested.

"If you want," she said, her mood having suddenly shifted. She grabbed her small bag and stepped into the bathroom, shutting the door.

Sean popped the cork and emptied the contents into the two wine glasses provided. A few minutes later Maya came back into the room wearing one of his old t-shirts. She climbed into bed. He walked to her side sat on the edge and handed her one of the glasses.

"Congratulations," he toasted.

"Thanks," she replied and set the glass down on the nightstand without taking a sip.

"It's bad luck not drink after a toast," he joked.

"That's bullshit," she chided.

He knew she'd say that. She always said that. Sean quickly undressed and crawled in bed behind her. After he turned off the light, he reached his hand around to touch her leg. Slowly he slid it up her thigh. When it reached her hip, he realized she wasn't wearing any panties, not even a thong. He was getting hard and he moved closer so she could feel it. He wanted her to know how much she excited him. He reached around to the front of her and where he'd normally find a bushy patch of pubic hair was now smooth. He halted momentarily, startled, but then he moved his hand lower to go between her legs.

"Sean, stop," she commanded.

He kissed her shoulder and tried again.

"Sean, I mean it. Stop."

He got out of bed and walked to the wall of windows. For a while he watched the taxis and pedestrians several floor below. With the lights coming from the marquees and electronic billboards he wondered if anyone could see him. He didn't care. There was nothing to see. He felt so emasculated, he was sure his dick was shriveled up and buried somewhere deep inside of him, instead of in her. At that moment he hated her. After an hour, and a few tears shed, he walked back to the bed, pulled on his underwear and a t-shirt and laid down on top of the covers. The pillow became a poor substitute for the warm hug he'd been craving.

As the neon lights gave way to daylight, Sean was up and showered. He was stuffing the last of his toiletries into his duffel, when Maya stirred in the bed.

"I'm leaving," he said. "Unless you want to make up for last night."

She hugged her pillow and said, "I just want to sleep."

"I just have one question," he said. "Why'd you shave your pussy?"

Talking into the pillow, she mumbled, "I just felt like it."

"It's just that you've always said women who did that weren't as sexy." Sean took a deep breath. "OK, I lied. I have a second question. Are you fucking Todd?"

She laughed, her face still in the pillow. "Sean, don't be silly. You're being paranoid. Just leave and let me sleep."

"Oh, I'm leaving alright. But I'm checking out and telling them the room is empty. So, you better get yourself out of here before the maid comes. You can crawl back to fucking Todd's bed to sleep."

She rolled over to look at him just as he stormed out the door.

Chapter 18:

Constance was up and gone by the time Greg woke. He made his way to the bathroom for a pee followed by a hot shower. When he came out, he saw that she had folded his shirt and placed it on his bag. He lifted and sniffed. It now had her scent on it, and he smiled before stuffing it into the bag. Downstairs, the doorman hailed him a cab for the airport.

He was fairly certain Sean would be flying out of Newark on a Delta flight, but he had to guess which one. Flirting with the attendant at the counter made his ticket exchange easy and free, and he was quickly on his way to the gate.

Greg proved he had gotten to know his friend well, when he spotted Sean in the waiting area. He moved in and took the empty seat next to Sean. Sean didn't look up from staring at his phone. Greg asked, "Where are you headed?"

"Minneapolis, like everybody else," replied Sean still not looking up and not realizing it was Greg.

Greg bumped Sean's shoulder with his own.

Startled, Sean said, "What the fuck?" before looking up to see his buddy. A smile replaced the grimace on Sean's face. "Ahh. What are you doing here?"

"Constance didn't need me for anything, but I figured you might." After a pause, Greg asked, "So how's it going? Did you get lucky last night?"

"Not even close," said Sean glumly. "You?"

"Same."

Sean nodded.

Greg continued, "So, I've got an idea."

"Yeah, what's that?" asked Sean.

"Let's head back into the city for the rest of the weekend."

"Gee, I don't know," said Sean. "I don't really have money to blow. I should probably keep my head down and get some work done on the damn house."

"A couple of days won't hurt," said Greg. "You need a break. Your arm is still healing."

"Are we going to tell our wives?"

"I won't if you won't," said Greg. "Constance is busy anyway. Does Maya care?"

"She definitely won't be happy I'm not working on the house."

Greg looked at Sean for an answer.

Sean hesitated, and Greg said, "I'll take that as a yes."

"Sure," agreed Sean. "After last night, fuck her."

"That bad?"

Sean's smile was gone when he answered, "Yeah." After a moment, he asked, "What about my ticket? It's nonrefundable."

"We'll figure it out," said Greg. "I'm on pretty good terms with a ticket agent out front. Let's get out of here."

It took some persuading but because they were nice and a flight on Monday afternoon was undersold, they got the exchange. They hopped in a cab and headed back to Manhattan.

"Where do you want to stay?" asked Greg opening a travel app on his phone.

"Anyplace other than where we were last night," said Sean. "Do you want to be by the tourist spots? I mean, what do you want to do? We should stay nearby so we aren't wasting time in trains and taxis."

"I kind of wanted to experience your New York," said Greg.

"What do you mean?"

"You're from here," said Greg. "I'm not. We have our place, but we don't venture out to other neighborhoods much. How about showing me where you lived, where you hung out, where you grew up?"

"Really?" asked Sean.

"Yeah, why not?" said Greg. "Hey is the bar you worked at still around? I'd love to see that."

Sean laughed, "No luck. It's an office tower now. But I do know another place with some colorful clientele and great burgers."

"Perfect," said Greg. "So, should we stay in midtown?"

"No, let's head to Soho."

Greg looked for Soho hotels on his phone, then rerouted the cab driver to downtown. They checked into a trendy boutique hotel. The room was small—two queen beds ate up most of the floorspace—but had a nice modern vibe and was well appointed. Best of all it had a cozy lobby bar and was close to Sean's old condo building.

"What do you want to do now?" asked Sean.

"You're supposed to be the tour guide here," answered Greg. "But how about some lunch and actually, I'd like to go shopping. I don't want to wear these track pants out tonight, and there's no way I'm squeezing back into the jeans I wore last night. My balls are still numb."

Sean laughed, then said, "My favorite Mexican place isn't too far from here and then we can catch a cab to Barneys."

"Well, I was thinking more like Gap or something, but if Barneys has jeans, let's go."

"Better yet," said Sean. If Gap is what you're looking for there's one over on Broadway and a few blocks north, a cool Bloomingdale's. We can walk."

"Lead the way."

A few hours later they were back in their room with a couple of shopping bags.

"These jeans feel so much better," exclaimed Greg. "You sure you don't mind me wearing your sweater?"

"Nah, it looks good on you. And I'm kind of psyched about my new shirt. I haven't splurged on anything new for a while." Sean checked himself out in the mirror.

"OK, grab your jacket. Let's do some sightseeing before dinner."

Their first stop was the Freedom Tower. Greg hadn't been to the site since the memorial pools had first opened. Since then the tower had been completed, the museum and transportation center. He was anxious to see them all. They rode the elevator to the observation deck at the top of the tower where Greg could see uptown to his own tower at the southwest corner of the park. They marveled at the Oculus above the train station. And they were moved by the images in the museum.

"Where were you?" asked Greg.

"Jr. High," said Sean. "We lived on Long Island at the time. Pretty much thought the world had ended."

"Did you know anyone directly impacted?"

"You mean in the towers? No. But kids in my class had uncles and cousins who were. How about you?"

"Final year of college in Oregon. Pretty much a world away. But it still hurt."

They looked around the exhibit for another thirty minutes until Greg put his hand on Sean's shoulder, saying, "I'm hungry. I think you said something about an awesome burger."

Sean looked at Greg's watch saying, "Yeah, I think it's about time."

It took twenty minutes to walk, but a few minutes before eight they stepped into Stella's. It was already crowded but they made their way to the bar. From the end, he heard "Little Sean."

Turning, she came into view, and Sean replied, "Stella." She grabbed Sean's hand and pulled him across the bar, and they pecked each other on the lips.

Looking to Greg, Stella said, "And who do we have here?"

"Stella, I'd like you to meet my good friend Greg, from Minneapolis." Then turning to Greg, "Greg, this is my sweetie, Stella."

Greg reached his hand across the bar. Stella took his hand. Greg immediately feared she would pull him across too, so lifted her hand and kissed it.

"A gentleman," she said with a wink. "And so handsome."

"Nice place you have here," he replied.

"I'm glad you like it." Greg tried to take his hand back, but Stella held on tight. "What are you boys up to tonight?"

Sean answered, "I told Greg about your burgers and we had to come here. Who do you have on stage tonight?"

"No one," she announced. "Gwen and Alice were scheduled but Alice's son was in an accident last night. He's pretty banged up."

"Too bad," said Sean. Turning to Greg, he added, "They're really good. It would have been fun to see them."

'But," said Stella in a voice loud enough for most of the bar to hear, I've got the karaoke machine fired up."

A cheer came up from the crowd.

"Sign up with Nicki." Then softer, just to the boys, "How about a duet for you two?"

"NO," proclaimed Greg. His hands went up. I just want a burger.

"I thought I was in charge here," said Sean. "You said you wanted a real New York experience."

"You haven't heard me sing," protested Greg.

"Not yet," said Sean. "But I'm about to."

"Can I at least have a beer, or ten, first?"

At that moment, Stella set two twenty-four-ounce mugs on the bar. "First one's on the house."

"Thanks, Stella," they said in unison as they took their first drink.

An hour later they had finished their burgers, another couple of beers and it was time for a tune.

Greg and Sean sang an abbreviated Bohemian Rhapsody. Sean carried most of the lyrics but was pleased to hear Greg didn't suck. A few of the ladies complained about the gay, or maybe straight guys on stage, fearing their haven might be overtaken. But most were gracious in their acceptance and applause.

"One more beer here," said Sean when they finished their song. "Then we have another stop to make."

"OK, but I've got to pee," said Greg. "I assume there's a men's room somewhere?"

"Yeah," Sean confirmed, straight-faced. "There's a bucket in the alley out back." Greg gave him a look of shock before Sean laughed and said, "Just kidding." He pointed, "It's back there. The door has a penis on it but don't be surprised if there are girls in there. I'm sure the urinal will be available though."

Two beers were waiting on the bar when Greg got back. "Man, that was brutal," he said. "You'd think they'd never seen a dick before."

"Some of them probably haven't," joked Sean. "My turn."

While Sean was gone, Stella, chatted with Greg. "So, you two been friends long?"

"Not really," said Greg. "We're neighbors in Minneapolis, so only a couple of months now."

"Really," she said. "You seem so comfortable with each other."

"We just kind of connected," said Greg. "He's a good guy."

"He is," she agreed. "I've known him a long time now. He'd come in here after his bartending shift. When it had gotten to be too much. He knew he wouldn't get hit on here."

"I bet he got hit on a lot," mused Greg.

"Do you know his wife?" asked Stella.

"Yeah, I met her last night," said Greg.

"I don't like her," said Stella, abruptly. "She's not good for him. Uppity twat from Connecticut."

Greg's eyebrows went up. And with the benefit of seventy-two ounces of beer in his body, he blurted, "Well, when I saw her, her bare nipples were in my face. Didn't seem particularly uppity, but I've never seen anything like it."

"You married?" she asked.

"Yeah, I am," he held up his left hand to show Stella his ring.

"Good for you," she said. "I hope you have better judgement than him."

"I'm pretty smitten with my wife," admitted Greg.

"He spent a lot of time in here before they got married. We talked about it. He was worried because her family didn't think he was worthy. Really shook his confidence. He was a hell of a musician. You heard him sing. He's good. And can play the guitar and piano. Write music. She bled that all out of him in support of her own art. He's happier tonight with you than I've ever seen him with her." She looked up. "Here he comes. Don't say anything, I just wanted you to know."

"Thanks, Stella."

"Even the urinal was in use," said Sean. "I had to go out back to the bucket."

"Seriously?" asked Greg.

"Not the bucket part," laughed Sean. "But there was a girl with her panties around her ankles trying to squat over the urinal." Looking at Stella, he added, "It's kind of a mess in there."

"Oh, like you boys don't spray your piss all over the place," she shot back.

"What got into her?" asked Sean, surprised.

"Oh, nothing," said Greg. "Drink your beer. And you said we had another stop?"

Sean pounded his beer, and they bid Stella a good night.

A six-block walk brought to a small neon sign and steep staircase leading underground. "This is one of my favorite little clubs," said Sean.

Inside a young woman sang an old ballad, accompanied by a small band—a guitar, saxophone, piano and drums. The crowd was a mix of younger and older. They were all dressed nicely and drank real cocktails.

"I thought you were more the metal and electronic type," said Greg.

145

"I like that too," said Sean. "But I'm really kind of an old soul." Pointing, Sean added, "There's a table over there. Want to stay for a drink?"

"Absolutely," said Greg, After the karaoke, this promised to be a pleasant respite.

They ended up closing the place down at 2 am and made their back to the hotel. While Sean was in the bathroom, Greg changed into the t-shirt and gym shorts he'd picked up at Bloomingdales. It had been a long time since he'd worn anything to bed, but then again, it was a long time since he'd slept in the same room with anyone but Constance—and even that was becoming rarer.

When Sean came out, he'd stripped to his underwear. Greg got a good look at the extent of Sean's ink—both arms, shoulders, left pec and around to the back. Greg wanted to know the full story, but sleep was calling. There'd always be tomorrow.

Sunday morning, they managed to drag themselves out of bed by ten. Greg showered first then offered to go to the lobby for coffee, even though neither was a regular coffee drinker. Once Sean was ready, they hopped in a cab headed for Brooklyn. Sean showed Greg where he'd spent most of his childhood, the loft where he and Maya lived before moving into the city, and the building where Maya was likely, at that moment, busy with her work.

They had lunch at Sean's favorite deli, before Greg said, "Let's head back. I want to show you my favorite spot in all of New York. The taxi dropped them at 79th and 5th Ave.

"You're not taking me to the Met, are you?" asked Sean. "I've spent way too much time in there."

"No. This way."

146

They made their way into the park and followed a path leading south. After ten minutes, down a rolling hill, they came upon Conservatory Water. "This is it," said Greg. "Have you spent any time here?"

"No," admitted Sean. "Central Park was never close to where I lived, so I haven't been here that much, except to go to the Met, the zoo, and a concert or two."

"When I'm stuck here in the summer," said Greg, "I like to come here and just watch the model boats. It's relatively quiet and tranquil."

They sat on one of the benches around the man-made pond. A handful of model sailboats circled in the water. Birds perched on the wall looking for bugs to eat. . .or better, popcorn from tourists.

"Have you ever sailed?" asked Sean.

"A bit, but not for a long time."

Sean looked at Greg wanting to hear more.

"Back home in Portland. A friend's family had a boat. I got invited along sometimes. As we got older, he and I would take it out on our own. Then when I got to L.A. I met a group who would charter a boat on weekends, and we'd go to Catalina. Once we all spent a week on the water in the British Virgin Islands."

"You must have liked it," said Sean. "What happened?"

"I did. But it's not Constance's thing. I miss being out on the water. I've rented kayaks on Lake Calhoun a few times— it's nice but not the same."

"I've never been on a sailboat," said Sean. "Looks fun though. I know what you mean about being on the water."

They sat for more than an hour in near silence, watching the boats. Finally, Sean broke from the trance, tapped Greg on the shoulder, saying, "Let's head back downtown. I've got an idea I think you're going to like."

They left the park and walked over to Fourth Avenue where they caught the southbound subway that dropped them at the Bowling Green station. As they walked into the Ferry Terminal, Sean said, "I bet you've never done this before."

"You'd be right," agreed Greg. "Where are we going?"

"What's the line? Oh, yeah, it's not the destination, it's the journey."

A few minutes later, they were standing at the rail as the ferry began its journey across the water.

"When you want to get away, you sit in the park and watch model boats. I come here."

Greg felt the moist breeze blow across his face. The ferry rocked gently as other boats passed.

"Does this help scratch that itch to be on the water?" asked Sean.

"It really does," said Greg. Then looking behind them, he viewed Manhattan as he never had before. "Wow."

"Maya and I did one of those pleasure cruises around the island," said Sean. "I like this much better."

When they arrived at Staten Island, they walked off the boat, paid their fare and got right back on. "Cheapest hour of entertainment in the city," remarked Sean.

"Well, not really," corrected Greg. "Watching the model boats is free. But this is a bargain I'll be trying again."

Greg pulled his phone from his pocket. "Shit. Missed call from Constance."

"Voicemail?" asked Sean.

"No, she rarely leaves one. I'm just supposed to know to call her back. I knew this was coming, but I'm about to lie to

148

my wife." He looked at the screen again. Then sounding relieved, "No signal. I have a reprieve til shore."

Sean turned his back to the railing, looking at Greg. "I have a question."

"OK," said Greg cautiously.

"I know I only met her briefly. And I don't even know you very well. But you and Constance. . .you don't seem like you have that much in common. How did you two come to be?"

"I told you how we met," said Greg.

"Yeah, I know that. And don't get me wrong, she's hot and rich. You met. You banged. I get that. But you've been together for ten years now. . ." Sean didn't know how to finish his question.

"What sustains us?" Greg suggested.

"Yeah, I guess. On paper, at least, Maya and I seem like a better fit. But I'm beginning to question that. We've been together less time and it already feels like we're changing away from each other."

"I don't know," admitted Greg. "Maybe it's age. Maybe it's life experiences. Our chemistry was off the charts when we met. She excited me. . .and not just sexually. That's tempered a bit over time. But now, she's my family. I guess it's as simple as that."

Sean turned back to the water. "OK, I get it." Then he pointed to the city ahead of them as the sun was setting. "Look at the lights coming on." After a minute, he added quietly, "I'm really happy for you that you've got Constance. And I look forward to getting to know her better."

Greg put his hand on Sean's shoulder. "I'm hungry. Where do you want to eat when we get off this tug?"

They found a restaurant not far from the hotel. As Greg was paying the bill, Sean said, "What do you want to do now? I know a bar just off of Times Square where the Broadway actors go on Sunday's after their curtain. The theaters are dark on Monday, so it's when they can party a bit. It's kind of an impromptu song fest."

"Sounds like fun," agreed Greg. "But the old guy is kind of tired. I vote for going back to the hotel, raiding the minibar, and you tell me what's going in those tattoos."

"And watch some hotel porn?"

"Maybe CNN," said Greg.

"Same thing," laughed Sean.

Chapter 19:

Sean hadn't been home thirty minutes before Katie Jo was standing at his screen door with a vase full of lilacs.

"Hey," he said holding the door open for her to enter. "What's up?"

"I picked these in the garden, and thought they'd brighten up the place a little."

"Gee, thanks," he said, taking the vase from her right hand. "What's that?" he asked, indicating her left.

"I want to hear about your weekend," she said. "And I had a taste for some prosecco, so I brought a bottle for us to share. Is that OK? Do you have time now?"

"Uh. Sure, I guess."

"Here," she said, handing him the bottle. "You open this while I go get some glasses. Then we can get settled in the library for a nice chat."

"You know where the glasses are," he confirmed.

"I've spent more time in this house than you have, my boy. Things haven't moved around much over the years."

She filled the glasses and Sean took a sip. Making a face, he said, "Kind of sweet." He set the glass on the coffee table. "Mind if I switch to scotch?"

"Of course not," she said. "Very manly and more bubbles for me. So how was Maya's show? Did you two have a fun weekend?"

He poured himself a scotch but did not fill the three other glasses in front of her. "Maya's show was interesting," Sean began. He showed her pictures on his phone of her three pieces. "This one is me. . .from behind."

"Oooooh. Nice. Did it sell?"

"All three of her pieces did. She was over the moon."

"I bet," said Katie Jo. "That must have made the rest of the weekend very fun." Her innuendo was clear.

"Ah, no. I mean, I had a fun weekend, but not with her." Katie Jo looked at him confused.

"She was pretty full of herself," he explained. "We fought a little. I decided to come back early. But then I ran into Greg at the airport and he asked me to show him around parts of New York he'd never been to. It was great and really took my mind off of the drama with Maya."

"Really," she said, in a long drawn out expression of disbelief.

"That sounds judgmental," he said.

"No," she said defensively. "Just surprised."

He hadn't really anticipated that reaction. . .or any reaction, really. But he knew he didn't want to get into it. He went to the desk and opened a drawer. He pulled out a joint which he held up, saying, "You don't mind?"

"No. Of course not."

"So, what did you and Greg do all weekend?"

Sean described the highlights. "You know, it's my hometown, so it's fun to show parts that tourists never see."

"But Greg and his wife have a home there. He's hardly a tourist."

"Yeah, but he's an Uptown Boy," mimicking the Billy Joel song. "I think he enjoyed seeing how real New Yorkers live." He took a long drag. "You spent much time in New York?"

"Oh, gee," she started. "When my husband, ex-husband, and I lived in Maine, we used to go down on weekends sometimes. I guess I thought I knew the city pretty well, but I guess I missed the local perspective. Sometimes I forget that people do live there. And not just wealthy people."

Katie Jo refilled her glass. Sean ordered a pizza.

"So, tell me about growing up in New York," said Katie Jo. And, so began the barrage of questions. After two hours, Sean was leaning back against the sofa with Katie Jo in the chair opposite. The pizza box sat empty on the table. "You ask a lot of questions," he said. "I'm beat."

"I'm just curious," was her only defense. "I probably should go though. Mother will be getting worried."

Sean took another sip of scotch, and said, "I want to meet her sometime."

"Who?"

"Your mother."

"Why?" she asked surprised.

Standing up, he said jokingly, "To find out how you turned out so weird."

Katie Jo just smiled without committing to anything, she made her way back across the lawn.

: : :

The next day, Sean and Greg regrouped to interview one more contractor, while in New York, Constance was meeting Maya for lunch.

The hostess led Maya to the table where Constance was already seated. The restaurant was in a lobby level space in one of the new high-rises on Madison. It was a cavernous space with high ceilings and massive modern chandeliers. The walls were covered in honey colored teak. The plush carpet

153

and linen tablecloths helped dampen the noise of the business crowd who frequented it.

"Ah, Maya," said Constance, standing to greet her guest. "Thank you so much for meeting with me."

"Hi again, Constance," replied Maya. "Thanks for sending the car to pick me up."

"I knew you were coming in from Brooklyn. I wanted to minimize the inconvenience." Constance took a sip of the white wine she'd already been served. Waving the waiter to the table, she pointed to the glass, saying, "Can we get you one?"

"Oh, yes. Please." Looking up at the waiter, she said, "A cabernet. Something peppery."

"You look lovely dear," remarked Constance. Maya was wearing black slacks, a white starched shirt and bright purple and red tapestry jacket. Her hair was tied up in a loose bun, she had on dark red lipstick and matching polish on her stubby nails—paint lined the creases in her fingers. Her only jewelry was the diamond earrings, and on her left hand, a narrow silver wedding band.

"Thank you," Maya replied self-consciously. "I wasn't sure what to wear. I love your dress, by the way. So springy." Constance was wearing a white, sleeveless dress with bright pink flowers exploding from the boat neck to hem.

The waiter returned with Maya's wine and handed them menus.

"Let's place our orders than we can talk business."

They took a minute or two to review the options.

"See anything you like?" asked Constance.

"I'm not sure. It all looks so good. What are you having?"

"I'll have the beet salad," Constance said to the waiter.

"Same for me," said Maya, handing him the menu.

After she watched the cute, young waiter walk away, Constance, turned her attention to Maya. "Let me tell you what I'm thinking."

"OK," replied Maya.

"I'm the top sales executive for a marketing company that specializes in cosmetics and skin care products for women. The products are very high quality and we market them direct to the end user through a home entertainment model."

"A party plan," said Maya. "I went to a lingerie party one of my girlfriends threw."

"Same general idea. Yes," confirmed Constance, a bit miffed at the comparison. "But if you came to one of our events, I think you'd see a significant difference."

"OK," said Maya, sounding skeptical.

"My company has fallen a few months behind on the introduction of a new line that I think will be very exciting for our clients. In the meantime, I'm trying out different approaches to make our events interesting so that we can keep our attendance up."

"And how do you see me helping with that?"

"I found your art—your subject matter really—to be very appealing. And I think my clients would as well. I'd like to have a small event at my place with about twenty ladies. In addition to promoting our products, I'd like to showcase one of your pieces and offer it for sale. This is a very upscale clientele and would be great visibility for you."

"But why me?" asked Maya.

"You're very talented, of course. And your subject matter. I just think my ladies would appreciate it."

"That's it?"

"Why so doubtful?"

"I don't know. It's just so out of the blue. You just met me."

"That's how opportunities work," said Constance trying not to sound as condescending as she was feeling. "It's a small world. I came to your show because our husbands have become such close friends. I liked your work. I see a mutual benefit. But if you don't see it, or don't want to try." Classic negotiating—dangle the prospect then threaten to take it away.

"No, I'm not saying I don't want to try. How would it work? I'd pay you a commission or something?"

"Oh, no, no, no. You come to the party. Interact with the guests. Show off your art. If someone buys, you keep the proceeds. I sell my product and provide my guests with some beautiful art to enjoy between sips of champagne and product samples."

"When are you thinking you'd want to try this?" asked Maya.

"I have parties scheduled all the time. I know you sold the three pieces at the gallery. Do you have others in your portfolio?"

"Honestly, the men are a fairly new subject for me. If you're looking for that specifically, I only have one other finished piece right now."

"Well, if it's something you're ready to show, we can schedule as soon as possible. I'd just like enough time to send out a tease to get some buzz going. Maybe in two weeks?"

"Let's give it a try. And thank you, Constance."

"Of course," she replied. "I'm anxious to see the reaction we get."

Over the course of their conversation, they had finished their salads and declined dessert. The waiter brought the bill.

"Let me ask you a question," Constance said to him.

"Yes, ma'am."

"You're very good. Do you only work days or are you on in the evening too?"

"Thank you." he replied. "Here, it's just days. But I also work catering jobs which are mostly at night."

Constance pulled out her business card. Writing on the back, she said, "I host a number of events each month—mostly in the evening. If you're ever looking for freelance work, call my assistant, Tina." As she signed the bill, Constance looked for his name. Spotting it, she added, "It's been a pleasure, Peter."

Eagerly, Peter replied, "Thank you again."

"I'll give Tina your name. I look forward to seeing you again. Don't disappoint me."

"I'll call her with my availability when I'm off later this afternoon."

As he walked away, Constance and Maya began to stand up. Looking at Maya, Constance said, "Opportunity."

Maya smiled, then asked, "Why him?"

"You heard me. He was a good server." Then Constance leaned into Maya's ear. "And his uniform fit his body—fitted shirt and tapered pants that hug his ass. It proved he knows how to use his assets for the maximum tip—which he received from me by the way. My clients will appreciate that."

Chapter 20:

Sean and Greg temporarily paused interviewing contractors and talked about other options. They even debated whether they could interest a TV remodeling show in the project but rejected it out of timing concerns and construction quality. In the meantime, they put all their energy back into removing the manifestations of the seventies makeover. Carpeting was pulled up. Paneling was taken down. With Sean's hand nearly healed, they even worked their way through replacing the broken windowpane.

Dirty and sweaty, they muscled a roll of green shag from the dining room down the steps to the dumpster parked on the street out front.

"It would have been so much easier if they could have put this behind the house," said Sean. "I still don't understand why they couldn't get in back there."

"Probably too hard to maneuver once it's full," offered Greg. "Think of it as leg workout day."

The two men hoisted the carpet over the lip of the green metal box and listened for the satisfying *thump* as it fell to the bottom.

Sean wiped his forehead with the back of his leather work glove and said, "I need a break. Water? Beer?"

"Uh, we have a couple more hours until quitting time, let's stick with water until then," said Greg. "But a break sounds good."

They poured fresh ice water from the pitcher in the fridge and walked out back. The tulips that were blooming in April and early May, were giving way to the flowering trees and lilacs that bordered the back yard. Sean wiped his nose. "I think I might have allergies."

"That sucks," said Greg.

"I'll live. But what does suck, is the way Maya has been acting."

"So, you're talking again?"

"Trying, I guess. I called her and she answered."

"That's a start," said Greg.

"I apologized for my outburst about Todd."

"Seems appropriate. Was she receptive?"

"She said so. But things are awkward. She's pretty distant."

"Maybe she's just distracted," suggested Greg. "The event with Constance is tonight. Maybe she's just excited . . .or nervous."

"Maybe."

"And it gives you a great reason to call her tomorrow and ask how it went. You know, play the role of the supportive husband."

"Fuck, that's all I do," moaned Sean. "When does she have to be the supportive wife."

"Maybe never. It might not be in her DNA." Greg lifted his glass to finish the water. "Let's get back to work. We can talk about this more over beer. OK?"

Sean was just about to answer when they both heard a loud knock on the front door, followed by a *hello*.

"That's a guy's voice," said Sean.

"So, not KJ for once," joked Greg.

Sean led the way to the front of the house. Standing in the screened opening stood an attractive man, probably mid-forties. Dark skin and hair. Slightly graying temples.

"Hi," said Sean. "Can I help you?"

"Hi," came the reply through the screen. "I'm sorry to bother you. My name is Manuel—Manny. I noticed your dumpster down at the curb."

Sean tensed up, worried there was city ordinance he was violating. "Yeah, the company said it was OK to leave it there."

"Oh yeah. There's no problem," Manny assured him. "Is this your house?"

"Uh, yeah?" said Sean hesitantly.

"How can we help you?" asked Greg.

"I just wanted to make sure I was talking to the owners."

"It's his house," interjected Greg quickly. "His and his wife's."

"I understand," said Manny. "Again, sorry to bother you. I'm very interested in this neighborhood. This house has been on my radar screen for a while. I know it recently changed hands and I've seen a number of different contractor vehicles parked in front. I'm making a huge assumption that the owners, you, are getting ready to rehab it. If all that is correct, do you mind telling me if you've chosen a contractor yet?"

"Uh, why?" said Sean cautiously.

"I may be able to help," replied Manny.

Sean looked at Greg.

"I think I can bring a lot to the project," added Manny.

Greg looked back at Sean, saying, "Maybe we should have him come in and tell us what he can do."

"Yeah, of course," said Sean. "Come on in." Sean opened the screen door, then asked, "Can I get you water or anything?"

"No, I'm good," assured Manny.

The three made their way into the library. Sean and Greg sat on the sofa, and Manny in the chair across the coffee table.

"Give us your pitch," said Greg in a friendly tone.

Manny looked a bit nervous, but his words came out clear and effortless. "I grew up not far from here, on the south end of the chain of lakes. A more modest home than this I assure you, but I spent a lot of time on the parkway, bike path, and paddling around on all the lakes. These old houses have always held an allure for me. But recently, too many of them are being torn down and replaced with new, behemoths. I get it. People have the money and these old places don't fit their lifestyle. But it still makes me sad because it feels like we're losing too much of the history. I'm not saying the new places aren't nice, but let's keep as much of the old as we can."

"That's my thinking," said Sean. Then he volunteered, "We even started by removing what we can from the makeover they did in the seventies."

"I saw the shag carpet," said Manny, with a smirk. "I've done my research on this house. I know it was in the same family since it was built. Until the last owner died."

"Still is in the family," said Greg. Manny looked surprised. "Sean is the grandson of the previous owner."

"I inherited it," added Sean.

"Congratulations," said Manny. "That didn't come up in my research." After a moment he said, "Oh, and I'm sorry about your grandfather."

Sean's impulse was to tell him he never met the old man but held back. He just nodded in appreciation.

Manny began his closing. "So, since you've started to do some work on the property, I'm assuming you're interested in saving it from the wrecking ball." He used the wrecking ball reference for extra drama.

"You are correct," said Sean. "I'd like to preserve the family history as much as possible."

"Great," said Manny.

Greg spoke up. "It's great that you're a fan of the neighborhood and want to preserve it, but why should Sean hire you? What's your company? What else have you done?"

"Fair questions," said Manny. For the next thirty minutes he told them why he should be their contractor. Then Sean gave him a tour of Chez Miller/Donaldson.

"Let us talk it over," said Sean.

"Absolutely," agreed Manny. "Here's my card. Give me a call if you have any questions. I really think we could save the history while making it more livable for today."

"That's the goal."

"Bye, and thanks for your time," said Manny as he turned to walk out the door.

Sean and Greg watched as he made his way to the pickup truck he'd parked behind the dumpster.

"I liked him," said Sean.

"Me too, said Greg. "Almost too good to be true though."

"What do you mean?"

"I don't know. Just the timing I guess." Greg slapped Sean's shoulder, saying, "Hey, we're not going to get anything more done today. I want to take a shower. How about you do the same and then come over to my place in an hour or so. We'll order Chinese or something—I'm sick of pizza—and hit the hot tub. We can talk about it then, after we've processed it a little."

"Yeah, sounds good," said Sean.

Chapter 21:

Maya entered the lobby of the high-rise on Columbus Circle just after five. Her name was on the guest list and the concierge directed her to the elevator to reach Constance's floor. In the elevator mirror, she checked her appearance— tapered black slacks, silk sweater cinched with a red belt, heels, and her diamond studs.

Constance answered the doorbell personally, dressed in a silvery blue cocktail dress that matched the color of her eyes. The neckline plunged to the belt at her waist.

"Wonderful, you're here," she said seeing Maya. "I'm anxious to see what you've brought."

Maya carried the canvas to the main room and spun it around for Constance to see.

"Oh, that's marvelous," remarked Constance. "Is this another of your friend Todd?"

Maya nodded yes.

Turning to the waiter setting up the bar, she said, "Peter, what do you think?"

Dressed in black jeans and a tight black t-shirt, Peter replied, "Yum!"

"Thank you," said Maya, beginning to blush at the praise.

"I have an easel over here near the bar," directed Constance.

"I want to thank you again," said Maya.

"This is going to benefit me as much as you," assured Constance. "Now let's take a look at what you're wearing." Constance took in Maya's outfit. "Peter, what do you think? Does she look more artist or schoolteacher?"

The waiter looked at the outfit, then at Maya's face. "I have to admit, your outfit is nice, but safe. It doesn't sync with the nude hunk in the painting."

"My thought exactly," said Constance. "You were so avant-garde for the gallery show."

"I wasn't comfortable going that direction for a party in your home," said Maya.

"Oh dear, regardless of the venue, you're still 'the artist'. Mind if I take a stab at a makeover?"

Constance was persuasive and Maya agreed. They went into the bedroom.

"Let me look in my closet at what might fit your tiny frame. Go ahead and get undressed." Constance was out of sight for several minutes. Finally, she came out, saying, "I have an idea." She crossed the room to another closet and came out a minute later with a white dress shirt. "This is Greg's. It's fitted so I think it might work." Maya was standing in her bra and lace thong. "Why don't you remove the bra," suggested Constance. As Maya unfastened it, Constance remarked, "I love your sassy, little tits. So much more interesting than the huge, fake breasts." Maya slid her arms into the shirt's sleeves and began to button it. "That looks great," said Constance. "The tapered part hits your hips perfectly." Constance began rolling up the sleeves, starting at the French cuff with the 'GP" embroidered on it. She stopped below the elbows. After a moment of hesitation, she continued rolling them to above the elbow. Then she unbuttoned the two buttons mid chest. "One more thing." Constance picked up Maya's own belt off the bed and wrapped it around her artist's waist before arranging the folds in the shirt. Turning Maya to the mirror, Constance asked, "What' do you think?"

"My Connecticut bred parents would have a heart attack," said Maya. "But I love it."

"Mind if I fluff your hair a bit? And maybe lose the wedding ring?" A few minutes later, with bigger hair and a naked finger, "Let's see what Peter thinks now."

"Sexy!" declared Peter.

"Maybe Peter would make a good subject," suggested Constance.

"I think he would," agreed Maya.

The doorbell rang, Peter popped the first cork, and said to Maya, "Hit me up. I'd love to pose."

Three hours later, Constance directed Peter to stop serving and over the course of the next thirty minutes ushered her guests out the door, declaring it to be a very successful event.

Maya had made a number of contacts. She had a list of names and addresses to notify for upcoming showings. And Marian, one of the evening's guests, was a gallery owner who wanted to see Maya's portfolio.

"Thank you, Peter," said Constance as he boxed up the empty champagne bottles. She handed him an envelope full of cash. "You did an excellent job. Just set the glasses on the counter and the boxes on the floor in the kitchen for the maid tomorrow."

Stuffing the envelope in his back pocket, Peter replied, "Thank you!" Then laughing a bit, he added, "Your friends sure are flirty."

"A bunch of horny bitches in unhappy marriages. They appreciate a handsome, smart, young man—they can ogle without getting themselves into trouble."

He smiled and blushed. "I'm happy to come back whenever."

"I've got a couple more next month. I'll let you know the dates."

"I should get changed," said Maya.

"Oh, just wear that home," said Constance. "I can get it back from you some other time." Maya began to protest, but Constance added, "I've put your clothes in a bag and I have a car waiting downstairs to take you back to Brooklyn. May I keep the painting for a few days. . .to enjoy?"

"Oh, OK," said Maya.

Constance was anxious to have the apartment to herself after a long evening. She sent Maya and Peter down the elevator together. A few minutes later she had changed into silk pajamas and was reclining on the loveseat in her bedroom with the night view of Central Park South outside her window. She dialed her phone.

"Hi, Connie," she heard through the speaker.

"Hey sexy. How are you doing?"

"Great. Is the party over? How did it go?"

"Really well, I think. Lots of orders. The women really seemed to enjoy Maya and her art—although I think next time, I should have her bring a few pieces."

"That's great." Then she heard his talking muffled.

"What did you say?" she asked.

"Oh, I was just telling Sean what you said about Maya. He's here in the hot tub with me."

"You're in the hot tub with Sean?" sounding more incredulous than she wanted.

"Yeah. We worked hard today, and I invited him over for a few beers and a soak."

"Oh. Well I'm sorry I disturbed you. I'll let you go."

"Wait. You're not disturbing us."

"Us?" Her voice was raised. "I'm hanging up now. Call me tomorrow if you can find the time."

"Wait. Constance. What's your problem?" She had already disconnected.

"Everything OK?" ask Sean.

Greg gently dropped the phone on the concrete behind him. He leaned his head back against the lip of the spa. The water bubbled over his shoulders and steam rose over his face. "Yeah. But she's in a mood."

"Should I go?"

"No," said Greg reengaging. "I'll call her in the morning when she's cooled down. Anyway, we're agreed on our opinion of Manny?"

"Yeah, I'd say so."

They tapped their beer cans together. Greg said, "Let's give him a call tomorrow."

Chapter 22:

"Oh, hi KJ," said Greg as he walked through Sean's front door. Looking at Sean, he said, "I got the juice and bagels." Turning back to Katie Jo, he added, "I only got the two, but you can have mine if you're hungry."

"My, quite the gentleman. Thanks, but I'm back on my diet for summer. No more drinking either."

"I was telling her about Manny," said Sean.

"Great. Any thoughts?" Greg asked Katie Jo.

"Oh, I don't have an opinion. Whatever you boys think is best. I'm just happy you're still moving toward a restoration versus a teardown."

"We all agree on that," confirmed Sean.

"I've got to get back to mother," said Katie Jo.

"Hey, when can we meet her?" asked Sean. "Seems like the neighborly thing to do, especially if things are going to get noisy around here."

"She's not up to visitors right now—but someday soon I'm sure. Bye-eee."

Sean took a juice bottle from Greg. "So, did you talk to Constance? Smooth everything over?"

"Yeah, we had a long chat. She apologized. Said she was tired and thought I was saying I'd rather hang with you than talk to her. It's better."

"But?"

"Oh, nothing," said Greg. "It's just disheartening when she gets jealous like this." He took a sip of his juice then asked, "Did you talk to Maya? It sounds like the party was a big success."

"Yeah, I called her, and she told me all about it. She's quite enamored with Constance."

"As is everyone," said Greg. "That's her magic."

"Well, Maya thinks that things are really going to take off now that she's making connections and her art is getting seen."

"That's great," said Greg. "Should take a little of the financial pressure off. Should we talk about Manny?"

As they ate their bagels, they confirmed they had heard the same thing. Manny was from a construction family. His father had founded a roofing company thirty years earlier and they had expanded into home remodeling—mid-market homes. Manny's older brother was positioned to take over that company and Manny was interested in building his own business. He loved the lakes area and the old-world houses and was interested in preserving as much as possible. But he needed a foothold to build his reputation and was willing to invest to make it happen. He, backed by his father, would front the money to remake Chez Miller/Donaldson. Sean would contribute what he could, and they would keep records of their respective investment. Sean would own the house, but if he chose to sell during construction or up to one year following completion, Manny would have first-right-of-refusal to purchase it outright at fair market value minus his investment, plus a significant interest rate. If Sean held onto the house for one year after completion, he would pay Manny back, with significant interest, through a mortgage on the property. Manny would document the construction and would use the house for marketing purposes throughout the process and beyond. It wasn't a great deal, for Sean, but it meant they had a way forward, and Sean could ensure that the house had a new lease on life.

"I checked with some of my colleagues in the real estate office," said Greg. "They know Manny and his dad's company. Good reputation all around."

"Thanks for doing that," said Sean. "Manny called this morning, so I told him to drop by with the contract after lunch."

"Pretty exciting," said Greg, lifting his juice bottle to toast Sean.

"Yeah," agreed Sean. "He said he's got some ideas for the interior layout now that he's seen the inside of the house."

"That's a good point," said Greg. "We need to make sure it's clear in the contract who has the final say in those decisions. Or at least how they get resolved. You definitely need to have a lawyer review it."

"I'll ask Andy to," said Sean. "Unless you have another suggestion."

"Good choice," said Greg. "From what you've said about him, Andy would be looking out for you."

Sean finished his bagel. "Feel like tearing down some paneling?" he asked.

Greg licked his own fingers, saying, "Sure. But one thing, first. Constance wants me back in New York for Memorial weekend. It's the start of the summer season in the Hamptons and she has some parties lined up. Mind if I go?"

"Seriously?" said Sean. "Of course, you should go."

"It sounds like Maya will be there for most of it too," admitted Greg.

"Even better," said Sean. "You can keep an eye on her to make sure she doesn't run off with some rich dude."

Would that really be so bad? thought Greg, thinking back to Stella's remarks.

Chapter 23:

Manny reviewed his ideas with Sean and Greg. He suggested that the exterior elevations remain unchanged. New, energy efficient windows, custom made to match, would replace the existing. The facade would receive new stucco. Inside the rooms at the front—living room, library and entry—would be restored to match the original after walls were opened up to accommodate and new central heating and cooling system. In the back rooms of the house, walls would be removed to create an open concept of dining, cooking and entertaining. Upstairs would be reconfigured, reducing the number of bedrooms but providing each with a modern, en suite bath. The roof would be patched, and a canopied terrace added to provide outdoor space to enjoy the lake view. The backyard was too small to allow for a pool, but Manny showed a sketch of a paver patio with a fire pit, outdoor kitchen with seating for lounging and dining.

Sean and Greg were both blown away by Manny's ideas. Manny handed Sean a copy of the draft contract before he left.

"Man, I love it," said Sean to Greg. "He just painted a vision that I could never have come up with."

"I agree," said Greg. "What he just showed us was more aggressive than I was expecting, but I think what this place needs." Greg fingered the contract. "Remember though, that the devil is in the details. Make sure that the contract specifies you get final say on the finishes. I like that kind of stuff, and I can get one of the designers from the office involved to give us suggestions if we don't love the direction Manny wants to go."

"I'll take any ideas you have," said Sean. "I have no experience in that kind of thing, and I don't really care that much."

"What do you mean?" asked Greg.

"Well, I just wanted to connect with my family a little bit. And preserve the legacy of this house. Remember, it's not like I'm going to be living here. I need to get back to Maya before this splits apart any further. Anyway, can you imagine what the taxes will be on this when it's done?"

The realization that Sean would be leaving when the house was done stabbed Greg in the heart. He paused to catch his breath before replying, "You're right. Let's just make sure we make it as appealing as possible to get the highest price from the new buyer."

"The way Manny has the contract set up—you know with the timeline—I'm pretty sure Manny's going to be buying me out at the end. It might as well have the finishes he picks. I'm just hoping to have enough money to get my condo back in New York and restart my life with Maya."

Sean was saying all the right things—for Sean. But suddenly Greg had a new realization and his priorities changed. Suddenly, heading to New York to spend time with Constance seemed more necessary than burden. He was reminded that she was his family and he needed to protect that.

: : :

Greg reviewed the contract from Manny, as did Andy. Aside from a few minor clarifications, both agreed that it was a fair document and reflected the deal that had been discussed. Sean signed it and had Maya's spousal proxy.

For the next two weeks things were a little strained between the two. Greg was more quiet than normal. Manny began the project management and less and less was available for Sean and Greg to contribute. Manny would assign them projects when asked, but he was also trying to move things along and stick to a schedule that their skills didn't mesh with. He assured them that once the project was further along there would be more for them to do, which, they assumed, meant painting.

The night before Greg was going to leave for New York, he was home packing. His summer wardrobe lived mostly in Minneapolis, so he needed to bring more with him for the long Memorial weekend—swim trunks, linen pants and jackets, sandals. When he finished packing, he went down to his man cave intending to watch a movie. He pulled out his stash. Looking at the joint he thought of Sean and said, "fuck it." He pocketed the joint and headed over to Sean's. Sean opened the door and Greg offered up the joint. "Want to get high?" he asked. They went into the library and took their positions at opposite ends of the couch, facing each other.

After a few puffs, Sean addressed the elephant in the room, saying, "You know, just because I'm not going to be living in this house forever doesn't mean we're not still going to be friends."

Greg responded, "Be careful. I'm going to hold you to that."

"You better," said Sean. "You spend plenty of time in New York. And we had such a great time there." He took another puff. "And if I'm around, and not keeping her boy out of sight,

1500 miles away, Constance might even grow to like me." He smiled a goofy grin. "I am pretty adorable."

"You are," agreed Greg, throwing a piece of lint he'd been picking at toward Sean. "What time is Manny coming in the morning?"

"Seven a.m., like clockwork." Sean stubbed out the joint. "This weed is making me sleepy. I need to get some zees."

"I don't want to go home," said Greg. "Can I sleep here?"

Sean smiled, but said nothing. He picked up one of the pillows behind his back and tossed to the Greg. "OK, but I can snore. You can't."

Greg tucked the pillow under his head. "No promises, buddy. No promises."

Chapter 24:

Greg's long weekend in New York and Long Island, turned into five weeks. Constance kept him busy by her side every evening. During the day he would spend time at the gym, run on the beach and work on his tan. Constance posted regular pictures of him and his progressing tan line to promote a new sun care product line the company had introduced. Sean followed her social media accounts and the posts gave him plenty of fodder to tease Greg whenever they talked by phone.

Sean's days were similarly productive. While Manny and the crew worked away on the house, Sean mainly tried to stay out of the way. He found a cheap gym to spend time in and rebuild his physique. He'd take a lawn chair across the street to the lake and work on his tan too. And he was reading. The few books that had been left in the library were classics. He had read some of them in school but never appreciated them. Now he was giving them another shot.

Greg finally came back to Minneapolis after the July fourth holiday. He dropped his bag and headed straight over to Sean's. His young friend was sitting on the front steps sipping a beer with a cold one at the ready for Greg.

Sean held out the beer, but instead of taking it, Greg grabbed Sean and gave him a hug. Initiating a hug was usually Sean's thing.

"Watch it," said Sean. "The neighbors will talk."

"The neighbors, like KJ?" joked Greg, standing back and accepting the beer. "Let her. How is she by the way?"

Sean began to sit back down but Greg stopped him. "Wait, wait, wait," he said. "Look at you. What's with the arms?" pointing to Sean's biceps. Sean grinned, proud of his gains. With his finger, Greg lifted the hem of Sean's t-shirt to expose tanned ab muscles that were not visible a month prior. Finally, Greg, put his finger on Sean's waistband, asking, "May I?" Sean nodded his consent and pulled the elastic down an inch revealing a tan line. "I thought you said you don't tan."

"I've had some time on my hands," said Sean. "And your wife's tanning line is quite good."

"Well you look great," complimented Greg.

"Thanks. So, do you." Sean held out his beer. Greg did the same and they clinked. "I've missed you."

"Me too," agreed Greg. "Now, back to KJ. What's going on there?"

"Well, with you out of pocket," said Sean, "I've spent a lot of evenings with her. . .drinking beer and eating cookies."

Greg gave him a puzzled look.

"Turns out her famous almond cookies are loaded with pot." Greg burst out laughing. Sean continued, "Most evenings we sit out back, either in her yard or mine, and get wasted."

"No wonder she's so fat," said Greg under his breath.

Sean nodded.

"Have you met the mother yet?" asked Greg.

"No. That's still a big mystery. A couple of weeks ago we were sitting in her backyard. I needed to pee so asked where the bathroom was and said I'd grab fresh beers on my way back. She sent me back to my house while she got the beers."

"Maybe she just didn't want to spook the old lady," said Greg.

"Maybe," agreed Sean. "But it's still fucking weird."

"Did she give you any more insight into your family?"

"Nothing big," said Sean. "Dad was a horn dog. She keeps trying to make me believe the two of them messed around. But then she gets quiet and changes her story."

"Do you believe her?"

"I guess," said Sean. "I kind of don't want to believe it, but she showed me a picture of herself back then. She was thin and cute. . .pretty doable."

Greg looked at his empty beer bottle, and said, "I need to pee. Are you going to send me home?"

Sean chuckled. "I actually do still have a working bathroom inside that I will let you use."

"Thank you, kind sir," said Greg, standing. "And then the tour of your progress?"

"Manny's progress, but yes."

They went inside. After Greg returned from the bathroom, Sean showed him around. In every room, walls and ceilings were opened up to install ventilation ducts, redo electrical, and add insulation. Windows that were standard sizes had been replaced while custom sizes were on order. The kitchen was still mainly intact, as was the library. The rest of the house was a maze of scaffolding, drop cloths and debris.

They made their way to the roof. "He got this finished before the big rains came last week," said Sean.

"Makes sense," said Greg. "Want to seal everything up before starting any finish work downstairs."

"And daddy owns a roofing company," said Sean. "So, Manny was a priority."

They walked to the parapet at the rear of the house. Down below, they saw Katie Jo walking across the yard with a six-pack of beer and plate of cookies. Both men started to laugh. Katie Jo heard them and looked up.

Sean yelled down. "We were just talking about you. Look who's home." He pointed to Greg who waved.

"I know. I saw," she yelled back. "Just a little something to celebrate."

"We'll be right down," yelled Sean.

"Man, you got anything smokable?" asked Greg. "I don't think I can eat enough cookies to get the buzz I want right now."

Sean patted Greg's shoulder. "No worries. I've got you covered."

For several hours the three neighbors sat around Sean's temporary backyard fire pit. They burned a mix of firewood and construction lumber to ward off mosquitos. Pizza was delivered and devoured in minutes.

Finally, Katie Jo asked the question. "So how long you back for, Greg?"

"Sick of me already?" joked Greg.

"No, of course not," said Katie Jo. "It's just Sean here, gets awfully lonely when you're gone. Puts a big burden me."

Greg looked at Sean to read how much of what she was saying was true. From Sean's face, he could tell Sean had missed him. "I should be here the rest of the summer," he said. "Definitely through July and Constance is planning on being here most of August."

"How did you swing that?" she asked.

"I don't know," he answered. "Time off for good behavior, I guess."

"Or good performance," she winked, being flirty.

It was dark. The sky was clear, and the stars were bright. Greg laid his head on the back of the chair and looked up. "Don't see that in New York."

179

"True," said Sean. Excitedly, he added, "I should get a telescope to set up on the roof once Manny gets the deck built up there."

"That would be fun," agreed Katie Jo.

"But you won't be staying here once the house is done," reminded Greg.

"Oh yeah," said Sean starting to laugh. "I forgot."

"He's trashed," Greg said to Katie Jo.

"I guess that's my cue to leave. Mother is probably wondering where I am anyway. Have a good night you two. I'll get the plate tomorrow."

"Come on, Sean," said Greg. "Good night, KJ."

"G'night, Katie Jo," said Sean.

She moved to him, brushed the hair from his forehead, kissed it whispering, "Good night my little boy."

Turning to Greg, Sean asked, "Will you sleep here tonight?"

Greg smiled and said, "If you want, sure."

Greg looked at his phone. "Shit!"

"What's wrong?" asked Sean.

"Constance called. Three times."

"Message?"

"No, but that just means she's pissed. I can't deal with her tonight. I'll just tell her I left my phone at the house when I came over here. And by the time I got home it was too late to call back." He tapped a few times on the screen. "There, I just texted her that and said I'd call her in the morning."

"And you told her you loved her, right?"

"No, because right now I don't." Sean stared at Greg. After a few seconds, he tapped again. "There. Happy now?"

"Not unhappy. Here's your pillow."

Chapter 25:

Over the next few weeks, the interior work continued quickly. Manny was hung up on permits for some of the larger projects, including the kitchen, but Sean and Greg could spend their days painting the rooms that had been returned to their original glory, now, with central air conditioning.

Constance was planning to spend all of August in Minneapolis, but plans changed. Instead she had been flying coast to coast and even to Europe, twice. Greg was headed back to New York to meet up with her.

Placing the lid back on the paint can, Greg said, "So, you think you're going to be able to get anything done without me?"

"Uh, I think I'll manage." After a pause, he added, "I will miss your stories though. May have to go back to listening to music."

"So, it's my last night in town for a while. What do you say, want to order a pizza and get high?"

Greg had been spending as much time on the opposite end of Sean's couch as in his own bed.

"Actually, I've got some stuff to do," said Sean hesitantly.

Greg looked at him, puzzled. "Seriously? Something that can't wait until tomorrow?"

Sean didn't immediately answer, but finally said, "The family is pissed at me."

Greg just shook his head, as if to say *What?*

"I mean it," said Sean. "I haven't said anything, but Granddad has been talking to me."

"What? Dreams?" said Greg.

"Yeah, and when I'm awake too."

"Too many paint fumes, my friend."

Sean looked at his paint covered hands.

"So, what is he pissed about?"

"He doesn't want me to sell the house. Says it needs to stay in the family."

"Hey, it's not being torn down," said Greg. "That's got to count for something." Putting the cover on the paint roller, he added, "And if your granddad is so worried about family, why did he let your dad abandon your mom and you?"

Sean was quiet.

"If you're having these thoughts . . . dreams . . . you know, visits from your dead grandfather, maybe you shouldn't be alone."

Sean didn't respond. He didn't make eye contact.

"Fine," said Greg.

"I'll see you in a couple of weeks . . . in New York . . . for Maya's show."

Greg tossed the roller onto the drop cloth. "Yeah. In the meantime, enjoy your conversations with the dead." He walked out of the room without another word. A minute later, Sean heard the screen door slam shut.

Greg wasn't sure whether he was hurt or pissed. Probably both. Regardless, he hadn't eaten since breakfast and he was starving. He ordered a pizza. Thirty minutes later the doorbell rang. When he answered the door, it was the same delivery guy he'd had several weeks earlier. His windbreaker was gone, and he stood on the steps in shorts and a nicely fitted blue polo shirt with the familiar logo on the left pec.

"Oh, hi," said Greg. "Dennis, right?"

"Hi," came a somewhat timid reply. "Yeah, Dennis."

182

"Uh, good to see you again."

"Thanks, here's your pizza." he handed it to Greg.

Greg had already paid for the pie online but handed Dennis a twenty as a generous tip. He took it but didn't immediately leave.

"Are you hungry?" asked Greg. "Do you want to come in?"

"Uh, I've got other deliveries to make."

"Sure."

After a moment, Dennis volunteered, "But I could come back later."

Greg considered the offer and its implications. Making a face, he replied, "Probably not a good idea." Holding up the pizza he added, "But, thanks again."

Dennis started to turn, but stopped. 'My old roommate is having a party. You should come . . . with me."

Greg hesitated.

Dennis continued, "I've got your number. I'll text you the details. Come if you can. It would be fun to hang out."

"Thanks," said Greg, stepping back into the house.

Finally, Dennis turned to make his way back to the car.

"Fun," said Greg to himself. "What are you Dennis, nineteen. Twenty? You can't even go to a bar. I could be your father." In that moment, Greg ignored the fact he had just been hit on by a college kid. He thought about the idea of having his own kids. When he married Constance, he put any idea of having a family out of his mind. But thinking back to his own college days. He was a wreck after his mother died. The amount of unprotected sex he'd had was frightening. Assuming he was fertile, having fathered a child was not at all unlikely. And maybe that was the case with Collin. Maybe Sean's dad never knew he existed, or at least not until much later. That brought him back to thinking about Sean. His disappointment resurfaced. Instead of spending the evening— night even— with this guy who'd become his best friend, he was back to being alone. Greg set the pizza on the patio table and retrieved a beer from the fridge. As he ate the first slice, he felt his phone vibrate. As promised, the text from Dennis with party details and a bonus—an underwear selfie. White CK briefs! Greg had to laugh. It was kind of fun getting hit on by a cute guy again. . .took him back to his L.A. days.

Chapter 26:

Greg pulled his canvas Jack Spade carry-on from the closet and tossed it on the unmade bed just as the doorbell rang. He grabbed his phone to see who it was on the front door camera.

"KJ," he mumbled. "What's she doing here?"

As the door opened, Katie Jo, said, "Hi Greg. Have a minute?"

"Ah, sure. Is Sean okay? I was just finishing packing. I need to leave for the airport in about ten minutes."

"Yeah, Sean is fine. . .as far as I know. I mean I haven't seen him since yesterday. I just want to tell you something."

"Uh, okay." Stepping across the threshold into the two-story foyer, Katie Jo couldn't help but sneak a peek at the formal rooms to the right and left with their floral print furniture and silk wallcoverings. "Come on back to the kitchen," added Greg.

Ushering her to the back of the house, Greg stood against the island, asking, "Can I get you anything?"

"No, I'm good." Katie Jo set her oversized purse on the marble surface. Pulling out a stool, "Mind if I sit down? I walked here."

It was only two blocks from her house and a relatively cool morning, but she was breathing hard and on her face was a light sweat. Greg reminded himself that's what carrying around extra weight does to the body. "My driver will be here soon, what was it you wanted to talk about?"

"I'm worried about Sean," she started.

"You just said he was okay," shot back Greg.

"Oh, I don't mean he's hurt or anything. It's just that he's so obsessed with his family. Do you know he talks to them? The portrait at least." After a pause, she added, "And I think he hears them respond."

Greg thought back to sitting in the library with Sean and pouring extra drinks for the men in the portrait. Fighting his own urges to let his mind run with it, he said, "I'm sure it's nothing. He's a creative guy with a vivid imagination. This is just how he's processing all this. It's a big deal to find out about a history you never knew you had."

"You're probably right," she agreed.

Greg looked at his Rolex not too subtly.

"I know you have to go," she said. "But there's something else."

"I've still got to finish packing," he said.

"I can sit with you while you do that," she offered.

Greg knew there was probably nothing more Katie Jo would like to see but their bedroom. Shutting that idea down, he said, "No, it can wait. What is it?"

She looked at the counter, her manicured nail tracing the veins in the stone. Looking back into Greg's eyes, she blurted, "There may be others."

"Other what," asked Greg, confused.

"Sean may have siblings."

"Huh?" was the only response he could muster. He had suspected Katie Jo had the capacity to exaggerate as they had been pouring over the photo albums. This seemed like more of the same. He didn't really have time to get into it, but he asked, "Why do you say that?"

"Collin was so handsome. . .and charming. We were great friends." Softly she added, "He was my first." Tears welled up in her eyes.

Greg thought back to the photos he'd seen of her as a teenager. Two neighbor kids learning about sex together seemed possible. He handed her a tissue, assuming she had more to say.

"We were so naive." She gulped, before saying, "I got pregnant."

"Really?" said Greg, incredulous.

She nodded, still looking down.

"So, what happened?" he asked. "I thought you didn't have any kids. Did you give the baby up for adoption?"

"Oh no. My mother wasn't going to bear the scandal. She arranged for a quick and quiet abortion. But I miscarried before the procedure."

"Oh, KJ, I'm so sorry." Not thinking, he looked at his watch again.

"Seriously?" she reprimanded. Then catching herself, she waved it off and said, "I know you have to go."

"No," he said. "Sorry, that was just a reflex. What was Collin's reaction to all this?"

"He didn't know. I never told him."

"What? Why didn't you tell him right then?"

"Oh, I wanted to. But my mother was very strict and kept me away from him. It was too late for me, but I wanted him to be careful with other girls."

"I'm sure he. . .well I don't know what I'm sure of. But he must have figured out about condoms and birth control eventually." Greg thought for a minute, before adding, "And from what you said, he was pretty messed up by the time Sean would have been conceived, so maybe not making the best choices." He looked at his watch again. "I'm sorry KJ, but I really do need to go."

"Wait," she commanded. "There's one more thing."

He let out a frustrated sigh. A text came through confirming his driver was outside. "My driver is here. Let me just tell him I'll be out in five." Greg typed the message. He set his phone on the counter and looked at Katie Jo.

"I knew your mother," she blurted. "I know I said I didn't, and I really didn't."

Greg was looking exasperated.

"But I knew of her. And I know she knew Collin. They were in the same class and I know they chummed around. I don't know if they ever dated. . .or anything else. She disappeared right after graduation. The story was she went to live with relatives in Portland—and go to school."

"We didn't have any relatives in Portland," said Greg, before wishing he hadn't shared that. He thought quickly through what she was implying, then said sharply, "Collin is not my father! My mom told me about my dad, and it wasn't him." Greg rapped his knuckles on the counter. He looked at Katie Jo, "Thanks for sharing all this KJ. I'm sorry you lost your baby. But I think you're letting your imagination run away. Now, I really do need to go."

He quickly led her back to the front door and guided her through to the front steps. Greg waved to the driver to indicate he'd be right out. "Take care, KJ."

Before she could respond, he closed the door and ran upstairs to finish packing. Without thinking he threw underwear and t-shirts into the duffel, knowing he'd have most anything else he'd need in his New York closet. He grabbed a sweater in case the plane was cold and a minute later the black Mercedes was heading up the parkway. From the back seat he saw Katie Jo walking back toward the home she shared with her mother. The abortion story flashed through his mind and he wondered if it was as far-fetched as the story she'd pitched about his own mother. But Constance and their trip to Amalfi quickly took over his thoughts.

Chapter 27:

As they rode the elevator up to the 22nd floor, Constance turned to Greg, softly saying, "I'm sorry."

He put his hand on her back and let it slide down to the curve of her ass to let her know everything was fine.

Once inside their apartment, she headed straight to the bedroom, tossing her purse onto bed while she continued walking toward her dressing room to remove her earrings. Greg entered the room, a few steps behind, pulling two roller bags.

"I'm hungry," he called into Constance. "Do you want anything?"

"I'm going to bed," she replied as she poked her head out through the doorway, showing she had removed her blouse. "I've got a busy day tomorrow."

He moved over to her and wrapped his arms around her. "I really did have a wonderful time with you. And next time. . ."

Before he could finish, she said, "And remember, tomorrow night is Maya's show."

Still holding her, Greg replied, "I know. I've talked to Sean about it."

"Of course, you have," she said pulling away and back to the privacy of her dressing room.

Ignoring her and leaving the room, he called back, "I'm going to see if we've got anything in the kitchen. If not, I'll order something. Let me know if you change your mind."

A few minutes later, Greg was standing at the Viking range stirring a pan of tomato soup straight from the can.

When it was properly warmed, he poured it into a ceramic bowl, picked up the spoon and walked to the window to look out on Columbus Circle below. The summer sun hadn't given way totally to the evening darkness. He thought back to their week in Italy. It hadn't been as *wonderful* as he'd claimed. Constance was asleep by the time Greg entered the bedroom. He quietly undressed and slipped between the sheets. The back of his hand rested against her satin nightgown, the warmth of her ass radiating through. For the next hour he watched the shadows from the street below dance on the ceiling before finally drifting off to sleep himself.

∶ ∶ ∶

Greg was already seated at the bar sipping a Cabernet when Sean came down the elevator. This time Sean had opted to stay at a trendy boutique hotel in the West Village, near the gallery featuring Maya's exhibit. When Sean walked into the bar, he immediately spotted Greg and worked his way through the happy hour crowd to take the stool next to him.

"Started without me I see," said Sean placing his hand on Greg's shoulder.

"Snooze you lose, buddy. What'll you have?" asked Greg.

Looking up at the bartender who had just walked up, Sean pointed to Greg's glass and said, "Same."

Sean stood back up and spread his arms, saying, "Come on."

Greg did the same and the two hugged for more than a few seconds.

"I missed you buddy," said Sean.

"Me too, Sean. Me too."

191

Back on their stools, Sean asked, "So how was your trip."

"Good, I guess," said Greg. "I mean. . ." he paused. "It's a long story. I'll tell you about it sometime, but tonight's about Maya. This shows a big deal. How's she doing? Have you seen her?"

"Yeah. I came in yesterday, and she stayed with me here last night. Today I met her at the gallery and got a preview."

"Is she nervous?"

"Not nervous," said Sean. "Excited for sure. Really the happiest I've seen her in a long time."

"So, things are good with you two?"

"I'd say so. We had a really good time last night. I was pretty horny. . .we both were, so that was fun. And then today, at the gallery, we just were clicking."

"That's awesome. How long are you staying?"

"I fly back to Minneapolis on Sunday." Hesitating for a moment, Sean added, "I have to work on Monday."

"Manny's got you doing stuff?"

"No. He pretty much kicked me out of the place. He needed to start working on the front rooms so I'm sleeping in the guest house now. It's pretty primitive. We moved the leather sofa back there. I've got a mini fridge and a microwave, so I'll survive. The portrait wouldn't fit so Manny's got it stored for now in the basement, but I've got a photo of it on my phone for my late-night chats."

"Still talking to the guys in the portrait?"

"Hey, you're not around. I need some drinking buddies." Sean held up his glass before taking a big gulp. "But I've got a better perspective on things now that it's in a mini version. I don't think you need to ship me off to the loony bin."

"That's a relief," joked Greg. "So, what do you mean you have to work?" asked Greg.

"I got a job," said Sean. Greg's look called for details. "I'm doing some project work for a marketing company in Minneapolis. . .on a contract basis."

"No shit," said Greg, too loud. "How long had this been going on? How'd you find it?"

"Just a couple of weeks. When I could see I was in Manny's way, I started looking at options online. I actually thought of just working at Starbucks but then I came across this opportunity. They liked my experience—and I guess my old firm didn't tell them I'd been fired—so they brought me on for a project and now I've got a couple more stacked up. The money is better than Starbucks—a lot better—so that makes it worth it. That's how I can afford this hotel," he chuckled. "And it's a good group of people. . .not assholes like my old place. Turns out I didn't hate the work, just the people. I'm having some fun with it. But of course, it's temporary."

"Damn," blurted Greg. "Quit reminding me you're leaving there to come back here. But that really is great. Shit's really coming together for you. I'd say I'm envious, but I think it's really more jealous."

"What's wrong?" asked Sean.

"Another time, my friend. Tonight, we celebrate you and Maya." Greg drank the last of his wine, saying, "Should we switch to scotch?"

The bartender poured two shots of Jameson. Sean and Greg held up their glasses.

"To happiness," said Sean.

They drank.

"So how much longer does Manny say he needs to complete the work?"

Sean laughed. "Oh, it will be months yet. Manny says three but I'm guessing four or five. It's a mess." Sean paused for a moment, then said, "But it won't matter if I don't have my favorite real estate agent close by to list it."

"Assuming you mean me," said Greg, "I'll be there when you need me." Quietly he added, "Whenever you need me."

Sean nodded, appreciating the sentiment, before saying, "We should get going."

"Okay," said Greg checking the glass for remnants of the scotch.

"Is Constance meeting you there?" asked Sean as they walked down the stairs to the street.

"That's the plan," said Greg. "But she's going to be late. . . as always these days."

Sean put his hand on Greg's shoulder as they turned down the sidewalk toward the gallery.

Chapter 28:

The mid-summer sun was casting long shadows on the cobblestone sidewalk when Sean and Greg stepped into the gallery. The space glowed from the stark lighting dotting the eighteen-foot ceilings. Black and white clad catering staff were arranging tables covered with buckets of ice stuffed with green bottles and crystal champagne flutes. A string quartet was setting up in the next room.

Maya spotted them immediately. A big smile illuminated her face and with arms spread wide she rushed toward them. First, she hugged Sean, then turning to Greg gave him a huge hug as well. Despite his surprise at her show of affection, he returned the hug. Feeling his squeeze, she whispered, "Sean adores you, and I want to get to know you better."

"Ditto," was the best response he had.

After, she stood back, she posed and did a model turn to fully display her attire. She was wearing a shocking red, halter jumpsuit, the deep vee neckline cut down to her navel. At the nadir of the vee, a large, jewel encrusted buckle cinched the matching fabric belt. Maya didn't have much for curves, but this outfit hugged her perfectly. Greg assumed it must be designer. . .and vintage. In her black stiletto heels, Greg noticed, she was nearly as tall as Sean, meaning she was now taller than him. And the distinctive red soles matched the dress. Her dark hair was smooth, severely parted down the center and pulled back into a low ponytail. On her hand she wore her simple silver wedding band and her only other accessories were the diamond encrusted platinum hoops in her ears. Greg recognized them from Constance's jewelry box.

195

"Fabulous," said Greg, in his best fashion critic tone.

"She's the real work of art here," boasted Sean.

"No shit," agreed Greg.

"I'm so glad you're here," gushed Maya. "Is Constance coming?"

"I'm sure she'll be here," answered Greg. "But she said she'd be a little late."

"I hope not too late. Most of the people invited tonight are from her contacts. Let me show you around."

They had only gotten through about half of the twenty-three paintings on display when other guests began arriving and she had to excuse herself. Greg and Sean continued on their own.

Standing in front of wall sized painting of two nude men poolside, Greg offered, "Reminds me of a more refined Hockney."

"Aren't you the smart-ass art know-it-all," joked Sean.

"Seriously, she is really talented."

"I think so." Sean beamed.

"Tell me, where does she find all these hot, muscular, well-hung men?"

"Looking?" asked Sean as a joke.

"Maybe," snorted Greg. "If Constance doesn't get her head out of her ass."

Sean grabbed Greg's forearm. "Something's obviously wrong between you two. Talk to me, man."

"I will. But not now." Turning his attention back to the painting in front of them. "Where does one find guys to pose nude?"

"They're models mostly. Some are art students at NYU and elsewhere. They don't charge a lot. Sometimes she photographs them and paints from the print, but she prefers to have them pose for the whole time if possible. I guess these two were pretty sunburned—in all the wrong places—by the time they were done."

"And she has access to a clothing optional pool?" asked Greg.

"At her parents'. Her mother was quite flustered at first, but I think she kind of liked it after a while," Sean said chuckling.

"Let's move on," said Greg. "The guy on the right is staring at me and I think he's starting to get hard."

Sean punched Greg's arm, "Perv."

Constance never showed up.

∴ ∴ ∴

Greg was sitting in the wing chair by the floor to ceiling window in their bedroom when Constance finally came home.

"What are you doing?" she asked when he turned to her and she spotted him.

Holding up a glass of mostly ice, he said, "Just having a night cap to cap off a very pleasant evening of art. What are you doing?"

"Don't start with me, Greg."

"Maya was very disappointed you didn't show up. Actually, probably more confused than anything. I mean, you set her up for this show, invited a whole slew of you contacts, dressed her up. . .and then you didn't even show up."

Constance wanted to avoid a fight. She began to remove her jewelry, ignoring Greg.

197

"She gave me these to return to you." He opened his hand to display the earrings. When she didn't say anything, he tossed them on the bed and turned back to the window. He took a sip of the remaining liquid in the glass, and softly asked, "Are you having an affair?"

"Fuck you, Greg," she shouted. "I'm the one who should be asking you that question. I'm working my ass off to provide a lifestyle to which you've become very accustomed. And you're sneaking off to be with Sean any chance you can. Spending romantic weekends in New York, right under my nose. And don't think I don't know you sleep over at his house in Minneapolis."

She knew about New York. But how? One of her friends must have seen him. Not that it had been in any way romantic as she'd claimed. But he hadn't told her. He owned that. How had she known about the nights he and Sean passed out on the sofa? Had Sean told Maya?

He knew it was the wrong thing, but he said, "Constance, you're not making any sense. I've been faithful to you since we met."

"I've seen how you two look at each other. I know Maya suspects something too."

"Sean's a friend. A good friend. I've missed that. But we are not having an affair."

"You already confessed about your past. Fucked every guy in West Hollywood. I should have written STD testing into our prenup."

"Low blow, Constance. Test me all you want. I've always been faithful. But lately you've checked out of this marriage. Our romantic Amalfi trip, we fucked, what? Twice?" His voice had grown steadily louder. He took a breath, before adding, "And even less time talking."

"That's not fair," she said, regaining some calm herself. "I've just been so busy with work."

"That's your choice Constance." Feeling defensive about his own work efforts, Greg lashed out. "I've been trying to build my real estate business for over a year. But whenever I get a new listing, I have to hand it off to another agent so I can follow you around the country to be ogled. I admit it was fun at first but when you accuse me of living off of you. . .well, I guess it's true, but not by choice." He turned toward the door. "This isn't a productive conversation. I'm going to sleep in the other room, and, tomorrow, if you have time, we can see where this goes."

"Wait! Greg, don't leave. Let's make love right now. I'm ready. I want to. I'm sorry. You're right. I should be more supportive of your career."

"Constance, this isn't some old movie where we fade from an epic fight into epic sex. This is real life." He looked at the ice in his glass, "Goodnight."

He closed the door behind him. She picked up the diamond hoops from the bed and threw them at the door, screaming, "Asshole!"

Chapter 29:

In the guest room, Greg couldn't sleep. He didn't even get
undressed, he just laid on the covers and followed the
shadows on the ceiling from a different angle. He finally
nodded off sometime after four. When he woke at nine,
Constance had already left the apartment. He needed to talk
to someone. He texted Sean.

To Sean: Hey bud. I know this is your last
full day with Maya, but I need to talk with
someone about Constance. Any chance you could
meet me for a late breakfast or early lunch?

A minute later Greg saw the typing icon and then the reply
popped up.

From Sean: I'll come your way. How about a
hot dog in the park?

To Sean: Perfect

From Sean: Columbus Circle Corner, 20 minutes

"That's pretty tasty," said Greg biting the hot dog they'd
purchased from the vendor along Central Park West. They'd
taken a seat on a bench near Greyshot Arch.

"Only the best for my boy," replied Sean with his own
mouth full of New York tube steak smothered in mustard and
sauerkraut. "So, what's going on?"

Greg continued to chew as he gathered his thoughts. "Constance and I had a big fight last night," he started. "She didn't come home until after midnight and I accused her of having an affair."

"Really," said Sean, surprised. "You think she's cheating on you?"

Greg contemplated the question. 'No," he answered. "But it was a big night for Maya. . .and Constance has been so involved in getting her to this point. Why would she flake out now?"

"Did you ask her?"

"Fuck. . .no," admitted Greg. "It was late. I'd been drinking. I just flew off the handle." Remembering the fight, he added, "But she threw it right back at me. She accused me of living a cushy life off of her hard work. She even said some nasty stuff about you."

"Shit, what did I do?" blurted Sean, taken aback. Regaining his focus, he said, "No. Not important. What about this morning? Did you talk?"

"No. I slept in the guest room. She was gone when I woke up."

"Did you try to call her? Or text?"

"No," said Greg. Sheepishly he continued, "My first impulse was to talk to you."

Sean put his arm around Greg's back and rested his hand on Greg's shoulder. He shook Greg, finally pulling him closer. "You've been married a lot longer than I have. But you need to talk to her."

"I'm afraid I don't want to."

"You're just going to give up on your marriage?"

"Maybe," said Greg softly. "I mean maybe that's what last night was about. My frustrations that have been bubbling for so long finally erupted like a volcano. You don't put the lid back on that."

Sean thought about what to say next. Finally, he took a deep breath, and said, "I'm really surprised you feel this way. I mean, I've seen you two and you seem great together. But I know what outsiders see can be very different from the reality of a relationship. I'm here for you and I'll support you whatever you decide to do. I still stick with my original statement. . .you need to talk to her. . .even if it's to tell her you don't want to be together."

"Fuck, fuck, fuck, fuck, fuck," said Greg rubbing his eyes with his palms.

"Without looking back up at Sean, he blurted, "She knows about the weekend you and I spent here together. Do you think she's having me followed?"

Again, surprised, Sean sat up to think about the question. Then noticing the rectangle form in Greg's front pocket, he said, "Dude, she's tracking your phone."

Now Greg looked at Sean and pulled the iPhone from his pocket. They both looked at the screen as it came to life.

"It makes sense," continued Sean. "It's a new phone. You said she had it configured for you. She must have had a tracking app added."

They looked through the apps not seeing anything incriminating.

"Nothing," said Greg.

"It must be hidden," said Sean. "That's the only thing that makes sense. But why?"

202

"Insecurity. Jealously. Control. Take your pick. What should I do? And don't tell me I need to talk to her about it. This changes everything."

"Well, it would be nice to know for sure before you say anything. The last thing you want to be now is the paranoid one." Sean pulled out his own phone swiping and tapping the screen for a minute.

"What are you doing?" asked Greg.

"I just made an appointment at the Apple store. Maybe a Genius can tell you for sure. In the meantime, I'd turn that thing off. Who knows what she has access to—camera, microphone, emails, messages."

"Now you sound like the paranoid one," said Greg trying to ease his own anxiety as he powered the phone down.

Twenty minutes later they were waiting for their turn at the Apple Store on Fifth Avenue.

"Thanks for coming with me. I hope Maya isn't going to be angry at me for pulling you into this," said Greg.

"If what we suspect is true, Maya is going to flip out. She really likes you and is happy we became friends. And she appreciates all the support that Constance has given her and the doors that have been opened, but she'd also been kind of suspicious of Constance's motives."

"What do you mean?" asked Greg. "Why?"

"Pretty early on, Constance told her to not let me get too close to you. She told her about your sexual history in L.A. and that you might be trying to steal me."

"That's absurd," said Greg. "Maya told you all this. When?"

"Well, let's just say I was in the know about your man-on-man activities before you got around to telling me. We didn't know whether to believe Constance. And it didn't matter to us whether you were gay or bi, or whatever. We liked you." Sean put his hand on Greg's shoulder. "And we still do."

"I'm sorry to put you through this," said Greg.

"Hey, don't worry about it," said Sean.

"I don't know why Constance has suddenly gotten so weird."

"She's an attractive, successful, wealthy woman with a hot husband who's ten years younger. She's had you under her thumb for all that time. . .willingly, I think. But in the last year you've begun to show some independence—getting your real estate license, trying to build a career, making new friends. Hidden insecurities can be revealed."

"Damn, you're pretty smart," remarked Greg.

"Nah, I just watch a lot of old movies," Sean laughed as his phone vibrated. "That's us. Let's find out what's going on inside your phone."

An hour later they walked out of the store with the original iPhone and a new one just purchased.

"I've never been a big fan of the Apple Geniuses before," said Greg. Too arrogant. . .but this guy really seemed to know what he was doing."

Brad, the *Genius*, had confirmed that a tracker had been added to the phone. He couldn't rule out other spying functions but was fairly sure it wasn't secretly recording audio or video. Brad offered to remove the tracker, but Greg told him to leave it. He bought a new iPhone, set up a new account, and a new phone number to give to Sean.

From the old iPhone, he sent a message to Constance.

To Constance: I think we should talk. .
.clear the air.

Greg was surprised when he received a reply almost
immediately.

From Constance: I need some time. You were
very hurtful!!! I'm going away for a while.
I'll be in touch in a few days.

"I've been hurtful!" shouted Greg under his breath. "With
three exclamation points. She's being her fucking manipulative
self. And I'm really getting tired of being told what a lousy
husband I am. Fuck that shit!"

Sean looked at the message. Trying to calm Greg, he said,
"Give her some space. Let her miss you. Then you two can talk
and figure out what's going on. . .and where you go from
here."

Greg sat down on the granite steps in front of the Apple
Store. Sean sat next to him.

"You should go see Maya," said Greg. "Get on with your
day together. I've somehow fucked up my marriage, I don't
want to fuck up yours too."

"Hey, I have an idea," said Sean. "Why don't you go home
and get cleaned up. Maybe take a nap if you can. Then
tonight, let's meet up at Stella's. I'll grab Maya—she's dying to
get to know you better. The three of us will have a greasy
burger, drink too much, have a good time and forget about all
this."

Chapter 30:

When Sean and Maya walked through the door of Stella's at eight—an hour before the first show—the place was already starting to get crowded. They spotted Greg at the bar talking with Stella and made their way over. Sean slapped Greg's shoulder, saying "Glad you made it."

"Hey, I've been here an hour already."

"Didn't we say eight?" confirmed Sean.

"Yeah, but I felt like chatting with my girl, Stella, here. Hi Maya."

Maya stepped into Greg sitting on the stool and hugged him.

"Great to see you, Maya. Sorry, I didn't get up," said Greg. "I'm afraid I'll lose my stool. Thanks for letting me crash your party."

"Don't be silly," said Maya. "And it sounds like you could use the distraction."

Greg looked at Sean. "I told her everything," said Sean.

Turning back to Maya, Greg said, "Then maybe you have some insight for me."

"All I can tell you is, I know Constance is crazy about you. Obsessed even. She doesn't want to lose you and I think she's worried that Sean was coming between you."

"That's crazy," said Greg.

"I know," assured Maya. "She got in my head a little bit too. . .about your friendship. But I'm glad you two guys found each other. Frankly, Sean's been much happier since you two met. He didn't really have any guy friends. . .or any friends for that matter."

"Me too," reflected Greg.

"Hey, Stella. Can we get a couple of beers here?" called Sean

Stella was furiously trying to keep up with the influx of orders. "Kind of busy right now Little Sean. I'm shorthanded tonight. Wait your turn."

Sean pointed with both hands toward the back of the bar, "May I?" he asked.

"It's not self-serve, Sean. Only come back here if you're ready to work.

Sean ducked under the bar top and through the passage. "Whadya need?"

"Two Tanqueray tonics," she said. "And a dry martini, three olives."

"Oooh, fancy drinks," he said.

Greg and Maya both watched Sean as he jumped into action. Sean was shaking the martini, when Greg called out, "I thought you were supposed to be a shirtless bartender."

Sean set the shaker down on the bar, pulled the button-up shirt he was wearing over his head and tossed it to Maya. Maya cackled as Sean poured the martini into the stemmed glass and skewered three olives.

"Look at that body," said Maya. "Now you can see why I fell in love with him."

"Not his big heart?" joked Greg.

"Oh, that was a bonus," she said. "A big one. But I knew I wanted to fuck him the first time I saw him pouring drinks. I was just praying he wasn't gay." She leaned her head in closer and chuckled a whispered, "He was a bartender in a gay bar after all, and a natural flirt."

"You seem really happy. That makes me smile for both of you."

By the time the show started, the place was packed. Stella and Sean were working hard to keep up. "I could use some help back here, buddy," called Sean.

Greg hesitated for a minute since his bartending experience was limited to cocktails he made for himself at home—which were always much stronger than any in a bar. But he figured he could at least pour beers, so he ducked under the bar to help.

"Um, I think you forgot something," said Sean, pointing to Greg's polo shirt. Greg hesitated again, but with Maya's encouragement, yanked it up by the collar and onto the bar in front of Maya.

After a few minutes he'd found his rhythm pouring beers with just the right amount of foam on top. He began to mimic Sean's moves and two were having fun playing off each other. From her stool, Maya watched, enjoying the show behind the bar as much as the one on stage.

At one point, slurring her words just slightly from the alcohol, "You know, except for the age and height difference . . .and Sean's tattoos, you two could be twins."

"I take that as a compliment," they both said, nearly in unison.

: : :

Despite his marital anxiety, Greg had slept really well. He had had a great time with Sean and Maya. He really liked her, and she had lived up to the praise from Sean. Also, working behind the bar had curbed his drinking time so he was not at all hungover. He was pretty sure Maya could not say the same thing.

Greg showered, determined to find something productive to do to salvage the weekend. He remembered the new underwear he'd brought from Minneapolis and retrieved the duffel bag from the closet. He reached in, pulled out the fresh designer boxer briefs, and noticed something else in the bag. It was the white t-shirt he had used several weeks earlier to stem the blood gushing from Sean's cut arm. It was still sealed in the plastic bag from the urgent care center. Greg had saved it thinking he might frame it—or something—as a memento for the work they'd done on the house. He had stashed it in the duffel, hiding it from Constance because he didn't want to have to explain it. When Manny took over the project, framing it seemed silly and he forgot it was there.

As he was deciding whether to just throw it down the trash chute, his new iPhone rang. He didn't have to look at the caller ID to know it was Sean, since Sean was to the only one with the number.

"Hey, Sean. Thanks for last night. I had a great time. Love, love, love Maya."

"Hey, Greg. First of all, Maya's mine, so hands off." Greg knew Sean was joking. "Second, we had a great time too. I'm pretty sure Maya feels the same way about you, so again, hands off. Third, if the real estate thing doesn't work out for you, you have a real future as a shirtless bartender. . .well, at least beertender.

"Give me a couple of lessons and I'll be mixing drinks as well as you," Greg joked back.

"Listen," said Sean. "I'm here are the airport in Newark, on my way back to Minneapolis."

"Okay," said Greg.

"Anyway, when I walked up my gate, I saw Constance sitting there. Like she was going to be on my flight, so I started to approach her to say "hi." But when she saw me. . .actually I think she was trying to pretend she didn't see. . .anyway, she took off."

"She ran away from you?" asked Greg.

"Well, she didn't really run. But it seemed pretty clear she didn't want to talk to me."

"She said she was going away. . .to get away from me. . . to think. I can't imagine she'd go to Minneapolis since I could easily show up there. Are you sure it was her?"

"Yeah. At least I think so. She's pretty distinctive looking. Although she was dressed more casually than I've ever seen."

"What do you mean?" asked Greg.

"Well, she was wearing jeans and a light, cotton sweater." Sean paused for a second, "And sneakers."

"Yeah, that doesn't sound like something she'd wear to fly."

"Unless she didn't want to be recognized," said Sean.

"Well, aren't you the sleuth," said Greg not really joking.

"She wasn't wearing much makeup either. I mean, she looked nice—pretty even—but not her usual glamor."

"Definitely doesn't sound like Constance. . .since every public outing is a selling opportunity."

"Unless she didn't want to be recognized," Sean repeated.

"Huh," was all the response Greg could muster.

"Listen, they're calling my row. I need to board."

"Let me know if she gets on the plane," said Greg. "If you see her again and can confirm it's her."

"Will do," said Sean.

"Have a safe flight."

Greg tossed the phone on the bed and looked again at the plastic bag in his hand.

Chapter 31:

"Oh my," mumbled Katie Jo as she tiptoed through the front foyer glimpsing for the first time the main parlor of the Miller house. The setting sun was being obscured by the storm clouds rolling in from the southwest. Through the dim light, she could still make out the details of the empty space. The coved ceiling and intricate moldings had been delicately restored. It took her back to being a teenager and hanging out with Collin. His father had let them take over this room to watch TV, play records and dance. They would pretend they were on American Bandstand. No other entertaining had taken place in the house for years.

She crossed to the library where similar details had been revived. Dad Miller had banned them from his private lair, but they had snuck in that night anyway. Looking at the empty bookshelves, she remembered them being filled and running her fingers across the leather-bound volumes. There was a crack of thunder and she was transported back to the night. Collin's dad was out for the evening.

The house was warm, and a humid breeze from the lake was wafting in, through the open window. Collin quietly poured some of his father's whiskey into a crystal lowball glass

"Wanna try?" he asked.

"What is it?"

"Whiskey," he said, taking a sip, gagging a bit.

She took the glass from his hand. Their fingers touched and she felt a spark she hadn't before. She took a sip, winced and had to quickly sit down on the tufted leather sofa.

Collin sat next to her retrieving the glass before she spilled any of the precious liquid. "Just like real grownups," he said. He leaned in and kissed her.

She was surprised. She wanted it, but after so many years of being neighbors and playmates, she'd assumed he wasn't interested. He talked about other girls and asked her about his chances with them. She tried to be encouraging but secretly hoped for him striking out. As far as she knew he hadn't dated anyone.

He gulped more of the whiskey before putting his hand on her breast. "Wanna do it? he asked.

"Do what?"

"IT. You know. Like grownups." He began grinding himself against her thigh. He'd slid his hand under her shorts to touch the elastic band of her panties.

She took another drink, herself and laid down on the sofa to submit.

Fondling her breasts through her bra he struggled to find the clasp but finally succeeded. He pulled off her sweater. He tickled her nipples with his tongue. She arched her back running her hands up his back under his shirt. He pulled his shirt over his head and laid down on her, their bare chests touching. Finally, he stood and removed his shorts. She could see the bulge in his white briefs. She undid her own shorts lifting her ass to remove them. He began to lower his briefs. She closed her eyes, afraid to watch. She felt his warm hands tug at her own panties. Again, she lifted her ass to assist. It fell back onto the leather. She felt one of the leather covered buttons near her tailbone.

She felt his skin against hers again. She kept her eyes closed. His penis was hard and felt impossibly large against her stomach. She panicked at the idea of THAT inside of her but

213

breathed deeper to relax as he slid down. It hurt as he entered her, and she gasped.

"You OK?" he asked.

Reassured by his concern but wanting to get it over with, she mumbled, "Uh huh."

She only remembered him thrusting a handful of times before she felt a warm goo dripping from her insides. She knew he had cum. She thought she had too. She must have. He rolled off reaching for the glass from the coffee table next to them. After he took a sip, she pulled the glass to her lips holding her forearms up to hide her exposed breasts. She sipped, tying to not let him see the tears in her eyes.

That was her first time. She was pretty sure it was his first time too, though he never confirmed. They did IT exactly four more times over the next two weeks before he began to avoid her. She thought they were entering a relationship but later feared he'd only used her to develop his technique. She ended up pregnant. Her mother was furious. A few days later, Katie Jo miscarried. She never told Collin of their never-to-be baby.

"What are you doing in here?" The terse question stirred her back to the present.

"Uh," she uttered trying to come up with a reasonable answer.

"You can't be in here. This is private property."

Recognizing the shadowed face behind the voice, she said, "You're Manny, right? Hi, I'm Katie Jo Larson. I'm a friend of Sean's. I live next door." She crossed to shake his hand.

Manny stayed put, holding the flashlight rather than return the handshake.

"Sean knows better than to let anyone in here. It's too dangerous. He's not allowed in here himself."

"Oh, he didn't let me in."

"Then how did you get in here?"

She'd come in through exterior basement stairwell. The lock wasn't working properly when she'd tried it. But rather than tell him that, she lied, saying, "Someone must have left the front door unlocked."

He looked suspicious since he'd locked up himself.

Attempting to distract him, she began her story. "I'm sorry about just coming in. I grew up next door and just couldn't help myself. You're doing such a beautiful job of bringing this old house back to life. Preparing it for another century really."

Manny didn't fall for her flattery. He figured she was harmless but needed her to leave. "Listen, we had to cut through a number of the floor joists to accommodate the new plumbing. We have new, steel joists and columns being fabricated. But until they're installed, it's just not safe to be walking around in here. That's why we've been concentrating the work on the exterior stucco for the past couple of weeks. Once it's safe, if Sean approves, I'd be happy to give you a tour of the progress."

She made her way to the front door. "Again, so sorry," she said as she exited.

Manny shined the flashlight around the library and then the parlor looking for any signs of foul play before making sure to lock the front door tightly.

Chapter 32:

From his window seat, Greg could see the lightening to the west as his plane approached Minneapolis. Calling in a few favors, he'd been able to get the lab tests rushed and was desperate to get back with the results. He gripped the manila envelope tight in his fingers and prayed the storm ahead wouldn't divert his plans.

Sean had gotten back hours earlier. Exhausted, he pulled down the shades, poured himself a tall scotch and crawled into bed in his rudimentary guest house. He had had enough socializing for a while, so he was anxious to avoid Katie Jo until he had rested. The sun hadn't even set yet when he drifted off to sleep.

A crack of thunder brought him back to consciousness. Looking at the clock, it was just after 11:00 p.m. He pulled up the covers and rolled over to sleep more, many hours more. He listened to the rain gently falling on the roof, beginning to doze off before an approaching siren stirred him again. Then another siren. And another. He sprang from the bed. Reaching for gym shorts and a t-shirt, he heard the sirens growing louder. . .and closer. He opened the door to see daylight. Only it wasn't daytime. But it was ever so bright. And hot. Fire.

He heard voices, authoritative voices, calling out commands. "Around back."

Two firefighters rounded the corner of his house with a hose. His house was on fire. They took up a position, back from the flames as other firemen rushed to join them. One of the firefighters spotted Sean and yelled at him to get back.

Sean ran around Katie Jo's to the front of his house to find out what was happening.

Several firetrucks and police cars lined the street. Flames were shooting out of the first-floor window and smoke poured from the roof.

"Oh my god," said Katie Jo running up next to Sean. "What happened?"

Katie Jo wore a rain slicker, while Sean had on only a t-shirt. Both were getting soaked but weren't sure if it was the rain or firehose or both. Sean began to shiver despite the warm air. Katie Jo hugged him but he wasn't cold, he was scared.

"You!" they both heard shouted. "Did you do this?" It was Manny running up to them pointing at Katie Jo.

"What?" she cried.

"So, it's just a coincidence that I found you inside a few hours ago and now my house is burning to the ground."

Sean was in shock, but he heard Manny's accusation, screaming, "She wouldn't do this to MY house. Yeah, it's MY house not yours."

"Read your contract, buddy," Manny said snidely. "Insurance claims are paid to me."

Sean shrank, remembering that contract detail that he'd decided was too obscure to fight.

Manny began to walk toward the fire chief to get an assessment. Katie Jo called after him, "How do you know the house wasn't struck by lightning?"

Manny turned back. "It doesn't matter. I've invested all the money. If I can't recoup it in a sale, I'll get it from insurance."

"Asshole," she mumbled.

"Thanks," Sean whispered.

The street was blocked by emergency vehicles. Greg's taxi couldn't get close, but he could see the flames from two blocks away. He ran as fast as he could to find out what was happening. He searched the sea of responders and neighbors before spotting Sean and Katie Jo.

Coming up behind them, he said, loudly, "What the fuck?" The rain had turned to mist.

"Buddy," cried Sean, grabbing Greg to pull him tight.

"You okay?" asked Greg.

"Yeah, I guess." Taking a deep breath, Sean stopped shaking. "I was asleep out back when I heard the sirens."

"Any idea what happened?" asked Greg.

"KJ says lightning," answered Sean.

"More likely that shady contractor looking for a payday," suggested Katie Jo.

"He collects any insurance," Sean said to Greg.

"That's suspicious," said Greg.

Just then the east wall collapsed into the structure sending smoke and ash into the air. Sean looked at Katie Jo.

"Is your house okay," he asked. "How about your mom?"

"Mom took her sleeping pill before ten. She's out til dawn. And I'm sure the firemen are making sure this doesn't spread." She stroked Sean's arm grateful for his concern for her while his own house burned.

Sean looked back at Greg. "What are you doing here?" he asked.

"I had some news I wanted to get back here to share with you."

"Good news I hope," said Sean. "I could use some good news."

"I think it's good news. But I don't think this isn't the best time."

"Don't fuck with me, buddy," growled Sean. "I'm having a shitty night. I desperately need a distraction."

Cautiously, Greg held the envelope out in front of Sean. Sean looked at it but didn't reach for it. Greg opened it and pulled out the official form, handing it to Sean. With the firelight behind him, Sean looked at it closely.

"What is this?" he asked.

"It turns out, that Mr. Collin Miller, before he had his way with your mom, he had his way with MY mom. This DNA test says that we are brothers. Well, half-brothers."

"I knew it," cried Katie Jo.

A stunned Sean looked at her.

"Look at you two," she said. "There may be ten years and a lot of miles between you, but you look alike. . .you act alike. Your mom's both passed through Collin's orbit. Too many coincidences."

Greg looked at Katie Jo, and said, "That's why you came to my house, isn't it?"

Katie Jo beamed with self-righteous pride.

Sean turned to Greg, "Are you sure?"

"This says there's a 96.2% likelihood," said Greg. "We can take test again. I used the blood you gushed onto my t-shirt, but we can have fresh blood tested. As far as I'm concerned, though, this just confirmed what I already knew inside."

It was too much for Sean. He slowly sank to the wet ground to sit. Greg and Katie Jo sat down on either side each with an arm around him. After a few minutes he turned to Greg, "I don't have half a house to give to you."

Greg slugged Sean's shoulder. "I don't want your stinking house. I just want you in my life."

Sean looked at the form and began to cry.

Greg and Katie Jo kept their arms around Sean until he settled down. Eventually, Greg said, "There's nothing we can do here. Let's go back to my house. Get you some dry clothes and a drink."

"KJ, want to come with us?" offered Greg.

"You guys go ahead," said Katie Jo, smiling.

"What about Constance?" asked Sean.

"You've seen her more recently than I have," answered Greg. "As far as I'm concerned, she's missing in action."

As they began to walk away, they heard one of the firemen call out, "It looks like there's a body in the basement."

"Just mannequins," Sean and Greg both shouted back.

Chapter 33: Epilog

Two days after Christmas, Sean stood with Maya, Greg and Katie Jo in front of his grandfather's house. All that remained was a burned-out facade—its resilience mocking them. A chain link fence had surrounded the property for months after the fire while investigators searched for clues to its origin. The insurance company pointed to arson, but the fire department, armed with eyewitness testimony from Katie Jo and her mother that the fire had started when the house was struck by lightning, ruled the cause inconclusive. This was a more favorable outcome for Manny and Sean.

Manny and Sean made up shortly after the fire. Both claimed stress for the outburst. In the end, Manny collected the insurance money for the losses and Sean retained ownership of the land, which he in turn sold to Manny.

Manny planned to build a new house on the property. All agreed the new house should have classic styling but bear no resemblance to the former structure.

Sean moved back to New York to be with Maya shortly after the fire. The agency he was consulting for in Minneapolis offered to let him work remotely with the prospect of opening a satellite office in the coming year. Greg had been to visit several times since, but hosted Christmas at his house. In addition to Sean and Maya, Katie Jo and her mother, Eileen, also attended. Eileen had become more social after finally meeting Sean and Greg. Being thin and stylish, with an acerbic wit, she was nothing like they had imagined. Eileen regretted Katie Jo's miscarriage, saying what a blessing a grandson would have been in her life. She was happy the house next door was gone, long claiming it was cursed—since her friend had died in the first fire.

As for Constance, she died in the fire. It turned out Manny had removed the mannequins weeks before and the body in the basement belonged to her. She died of smoke inhalation, but the investigators were not sure why she was there. She had apparently become overcome by the smoke shortly after the fire had ignited. And the lighter found near her body, that the fire department had assumed belonged to a worker, was the same one from her father that she used to light the fireplaces in the house. Greg knew what had happened. The fire hadn't been started by lightning, but he was happy to let them believe so.

Constance had left a financial mess for Greg to dig through. They were deeply in debt. She had borrowed against the house and New York condo to help keep her failing employer afloat when they were too slow to adapt to a social media economy and business model. With the money she had poured into the business, she owned nearly forty percent of it. For all intents and purposes, she had become the face of the brand and when the news came out of her death, the company quickly filed bankruptcy and liquidated the few remaining assets. Greg got nothing. His lawyer negotiated for him to be able to stay in the house until it sold. The Christmas gathering was his last hurrah. It hadn't yet sold, but he was done with it and ready to move on.

Manny's workers maneuvered the backhoe into position, ready to topple the remaining facade to clear the land for the new house. He agreed that the new family portrait, which Maya was painting to include Sean and Greg—as well as a secret reference to Katie Jo's unborn child—would hang in the new library for staging. All the Miller/Donaldson/Piersol/ Larson men would finally be together.

"We should probably be getting to the airport," said Sean.

"Thanks for having us," added Maya.

Greg put his arm around Sean, saying, "I'm so glad we finally got to spend a Christmas together."

Both started to tear up.

"Just one of many," said Sean.

"And I'll be in New York on Friday to spend New Year's with you guys," added Greg.

"Before you start your big travel adventure," added Maya.

"Before I have to get a job," Greg said. "I'm going to try to make my savings last for a year—visit some national parks, see Thailand, finally hit Burning Man—but the money isn't going last much longer than that."

"What about your portion of the proceeds from Granddad's land?" asked Sean.

"Retirement account," answered Greg. "I need to start being responsible at my age."

Katie Jo stood by, quietly wringing her hands. She began to sob.

Sean grabbed her, pulling her close, asking, "What's wrong, KJ?"

"I'm just so worried I'm never going to see you again. You two are like my own boys." Tears were flowing and freezing on her cheeks.

"Of course, you will," said Sean and Greg in unison.

"You're part of the this fucked up family too," said Sean. "Don't you ever forget it!"

"You like New York, right?" asked Maya. Katie Jo nodded. "When we get our new place, we'll have plenty of room for guests."

Katie Jo let herself be drawn into a group hug.

"Let's get you guys to your flight," said Greg. They made their way toward Greg's Jaguar, one of his few personal possessions not caught up in Constance's folly.

Before they got in the car, Sean asked, "Do you miss her?"

"Yes," Greg replied without hesitation. "I've had a lot of time to think about it. I loved her. I saw behind the facade. I hate what she tried to do. I blame the collapse of her business. It made her crazy. But in the end, she loved me when I had no one else."

"You make it sound like it was a burden for her to love you," said Maya. "I assure you it is not. And let's not forget she tried to kill Sean," she added defensively.

Greg's eyes narrowed as he looked at her. Then he looked at Sean.

Maya looked at Sean, worried she'd crossed the line with Greg. She wasn't sure if he was about to explode with anger or cry.

Sean debated whether to add anything.

After an uncomfortably long a pause, Greg said, "You're right! She won my heart, then betrayed me. I'm sorry she died." Turning to Sean, he added, "But if she had hurt you, I would have killed her." Greg wrapped Maya in his left arm and Sean in his right. "Thanks. Now it's time to get my family to the airport."

::: The End :::

Made in the USA
Columbia, SC
12 January 2020

86676876R00124